Snowball
and Other Stories

Snowball the Pony
and Other Stories

Snowball the Pony
Enid Blyton
Illustrations by Jan Lewis

Bimbo and Topsy
Enid Blyton
Illustrations by Guy Parker-Rees

Run-About's Holiday
Enid Blyton
Illustrations by Brian Lee

BLOOMSBURY
CHILDREN'S
BOOKS

First published by Parragon Publishing in 1999
Queen Street House, 4/5 Queen Street, Bath BA1 1HE

Snowball the Pony was first published by Lutterworth Press in 1953
Bimbo and Topsy was first published by Newnes in 1943
Run-About's Holiday was first published by Lutterworth Press in 1955
First published by Bloomsbury Publishing Plc in 1997
38 Soho Square, London, W1V 5DF

Enid Blyton

The moral right of the author has been asserted
A CIP catalogue record of this book is available from the
British Library

ISBN 1 84164 091 3

Printed in Scotland by Caledonian International Book Manufacturing Ltd

10 9 8 7 6 5 4 3 2 1

Cover Design by Mandy Sherliker

Contents

Snowball the Pony

Snowball the Pony

Enid Blyton
Illustrations by Jan Lewis

BLOOMSBURY
CHILDREN'S
BOOKS

Contents

Chapter 1
The Little Black Pony

A tiny pony stood by his mother in the corner of a field. He was so small that he wasn't much bigger than a big dog.

He had no name yet. The farmer he belonged to meant to sell him, so he hadn't bothered to give him a name.

He was black all over, as black as soot, and he had a nice long tail that he could whisk about, and bright eyes that noticed everything. His coat was like black satin, and his nose was as soft as velvet.

He was beautiful, and every child who saw him loved him and wanted him, but he was a wild little thing and wouldn't go near any boy or girl who called to him.

He loved his mother, and she loved him.

She often rubbed him softly with her nose, and he stood close to her to feel her warm, soft body. They lived in a big field together, and often liked to gallop round it.

'Have you lived here a long time, Mother?' said the little pony one day. 'All your life long?'

'Not all my life long,' said his mother. 'Most of it. I came here when I was very, very small, as small as you. I was given to the little boy, and I was his pony. He rode me for a long time, but now he is almost grown-up.'

'Who will ride *me*?' said the little pony, looking at his mother with big bright eyes.

'I don't know,' said his mother. 'There are no children here. The farmer may sell you, and you may go far, far away.'

'I don't want to,' said the little pony, and he pressed closely against his mother. 'I want to stay with you in this lovely sunny field always and always.'

'You won't be able to do that,' said his mother. 'It wouldn't be good for you. You must learn many things; you must go out into the big world; you must have a master; and you must grow up into a fine pony, loyal and obedient.'

'I don't want to,' said the tiny pony, in alarm. 'I should be afraid to leave you. Don't let me go away, Mother!'

'Well, you won't go yet,' said his mother. 'You are too small. Now let's go for a canter round the field and see if we can find where the grass grows long and juicy in the ditch.'

So they cantered off together, the little pony keeping close to his mother's side. They found the grass and nibbled it in delight. It was much nicer than the short grass in the field.

The farmer came to look at the tiny black pony a few days afterwards. His wife was with him.

'How lovely he is!' she cried. 'He looks like a toy pony! I wish we could keep him.'

'No, we must sell him,' said the farmer. 'He will bring joy to some child, who will ride him and love him. What a dear little fellow he is! I shall sell him next summer, but I will choose someone kind for him. He shall not go to any spoilt child who might whip him.'

'There! Did you hear that? You will soon be sold,' said the pony's mother. 'I shall miss you. But it will be nice for you to have your own home and a little master to love. The best thing in the world is to love and be loved, little pony, so be kind to everyone and make as many friends as you can.'

The little pony grew well in the next few months. How his black coat shone! There was nothing white about him at all except for a few hairs in his tail, and nobody ever noticed those.

'I expect you will be called Sooty or Blackie or Cinders,' said his mother. 'You are so very black.'

Soon the time came for him to be sold. He was to go the very next day. He was sad and kept close to his mother.

'Now don't worry,' she said to him. 'You will be quite all right. Always obey your master; always be kind; and take great care of any children who ride you.'

'Shan't I ever see you again?' said the little pony, sadly. 'I shall miss you so much.'

'Well, you are not going very far away,' said his mother. 'You are going to the children who live on the next farm to ours. So, perhaps some day you will be able to come over and see me. Maybe the children will ride you over here.'

'Oh, that will be lovely,' said the little pony. He began to feel excited. He was going out into the big world. How big was it? He didn't know, because he had never been out of the field-gate. He thought the world might be as far as the hills he could see.

The next day the farmer came, and, after giving the pony some oats, slipped a halter on to lead him away. He nuzzled against his mother for the last time and she rubbed him gently with her nose.

'Be good; be kind; do as you are told,' she

said. 'Then you will be happy. Goodbye, little pony.'

'Goodbye,' said the pony, and trotted out of the gate very sadly. It swung to and closed with a click. Now, for the first time, he was on the other side of the gate. The lane stretched out before him, looking very long.

The world seemed very big and very strange.

'Come along,' said the farmer. 'We are going to your new home.'

And off they went, the little pony looking round him with big, astonished eyes.

Chapter 2

A New Home and a New Name

The little pony was surprised to find how big the world was. The lane was a long one and led into a main road, which seemed enormous to the little creature.

He jogged along by the farmer, looking in astonishment at the houses they passed. He had only seen the farmhouse before far away in the distance. Then suddenly a great red animal roared by, and the tiny pony leapt in fright, trying to jump into the ditch to hide.

'What's that?' he thought. 'Will it eat me, oh will it eat me?'

'Now, now,' said the farmer, laughing, 'that was only a bus. It won't hurt you! Come along.'

Soon they left the main road and went into another lane. This led over the blue hills that the pony had so often seen from his field. He saw cornfields on each side, growing green, with a poppy or two flashing a red eye at him now and again.

They came to the top of the hill and the pony looked in surprise at the valley below. Why, the world was even bigger than he had thought! It was an enormous place!

'Now, there's your new home, down there,' said the farmer, and he nodded at a pretty farmhouse nestling down in the valley. 'You'll like living there. There are three children to ride you, and they're nice children, so don't you try any silly tricks with them.'

The pony pricked up his ears. Three children! He would like that. He was shy of boys and girls, but once he knew them it would be great fun to play with them. He jogged on happily, feeling more and more excited.

They came to the farm. A little white gate led to the farmhouse. Swinging on it were three children, waiting for them. They saw the tiny pony and shouted in delight.

'There he is! Look, there he comes! Oh, isn't he sweet? He's the nicest little pony we've ever seen!'

They jumped off the gate and rushed to meet the farmer and the pony. He was afraid and ran back, nearly pulling the rope from the farmer's hand. But the farmer pushed him forward.

'What, you're shy! Don't be silly! Just show how beautiful you are!'

'He *is* beautiful,' said Willie, a big boy of ten. 'The most beautiful pony I've ever seen.'

'Oh the darling!' said Sheila, who was seven, and she put her arms round his neck.

'I want to ride him now, now, now!' cried Timmy, the youngest. He was five. The farmer lifted him up and put him on the pony's back, holding him there. The pony jumped in fright. He was not used to having anyone on his back, and he didn't like it.

'Now, now!' said the farmer. 'You'll have to get used to this. Well, Timmy, how do you like him?'

'I love him,' said Timmy, his round face red with joy. 'Take me off again. I want to look at him.'

'Well, I must leave him now,' said the farmer. 'Where's he to be kept?'

'In the field just here,' said Willie, and he pointed to the field near the farmhouse garden. 'I'll take him. Oh, isn't he lovely? Has he got a name?'

'No,' said the farmer, giving the rope to Willie to lead the pony away. 'I left it to you children to name him. Well, I hope he'll be good. He's a dear little fellow. Now I'll go and have a word with your father. I can see him in the fields up above.'

He left the pony with the children. They led him into the field and shut the gate. He stood and looked at them with his bright, puzzled eyes. Everything was so strange to him. He wanted his mother there.

'You're the dearest pony in the world, and you're ours!' said Sheila, rubbing his nose gently. 'But first we must give you a name.'

'*Not* Sooty or Blackie or Cinders,' said Willie.

'But he's *very* black!' said Sheila. 'We ought to call him something black.'

'I don't like black names,' said Willie. 'I shan't call him a black name.'

'Oh well, call him Snowball or Snow-white

24

or Snowdrop!' said Sheila, laughing. The others stared and Willie laughed too.

'Good idea! We'll call him Snowball! That will make people laugh. Anyway, it's a nice name. Snowball, do you like your new name?'

The pony turned his head to Willie. He liked Willie. He didn't know what a snowball was. He had never seen snow. He thought it was a nice name, and he was very glad to have a name of his own. He hoped his mother would like it too.

'Snowball!' said Sheila, softly, in his ear. 'That's your name, little pony. Snowball! Now, when you hear us calling that, you must always come trotting over to us. See?'

'Snowball,' said Timmy, and he patted the pony on the neck. 'You're a black snowball, and you're ours and we love you.'

'We won't try to ride him today,' said Willie. 'He's shy and frightened because he's been brought away from his home. We'll just talk to him and trot him about. He'll soon settle down and be happy!'

'Come along, Snowball, come round the field,' said Sheila.

And Snowball trotted off with the three children in delight.

Chapter 3
Snowball's Field

Soon the children went in to their dinner, and their mother heard all about Snowball. She promised to go out and see him afterwards.

'He will be a lovely pet for you,' she said, 'and even Timmy will be able to ride him. I think Daddy is bringing tack for him today, because soon he will have to learn how to carry a saddle, and obey the reins.'

'He won't like that at first,' said Willie. 'But he will soon get used to it. He's so sweet, Mother. I've never seen such a lovely pony. His coat is like gleaming black satin.'

'Whatever made you call him Snowball?' said his mother, smiling. 'That's a good joke!'

'I hope he's not feeling very lonely in the field by himself,' said Sheila. 'I expect he's missing his mother very much.'

Snowball was feeling very lonely. He wanted the children to come and talk to him again. Where had they gone and when would they come back?

He nibbled some grass and it tasted rather nice. He wandered round the field, and felt proud to think it was *his* field. There was no other creature in it. There were cows in the next field, and sheep on the hill side. But he was the only creature in his own field.

But what was this? A brown hen came through the hedge and began to peck at the ground in his field. Then another hen came and another. Snowball stood and looked at them angrily.

'This is *my* field!' he neighed to them and he ran up fiercely. The first brown hen looked surprised.

'*Your* field? What do you mean? We always come in here to peck about. Don't be silly.'

'Go away,' said Snowball. 'I won't have you here!' He ran at the hen and she scuttled back into the hedge. Then he ran at the other two, and they went off as well. But no sooner had he turned his back than the first hen came back again through another hole further off.

Snowball was cross. He trotted over to the hen and she gave a cluck and ran off – but just as she went into the hedge some more hens came in at the opposite side of the field. Snowball galloped across to tell them what he thought of them.

Soon the hens were having a fine game with the little pony. 'Can't catch *me*! Can't catch *me*!' first one hen clucked and then another. Snowball dashed at them all, and then he stamped his hoof.

'I shall tell the children! You know this is my field, and I don't allow anyone else in it.'

A big brown horse looked over the hedge, and stared at Snowball. 'Hello!' he said. 'I haven't seen you before. What's all this fuss about?'

'It's these hens,' said Snowball. 'It's the first time I've had a field of my own, and I don't want hens in it.'

'This isn't your field,' said the big brown horse. 'It's only the field where you are allowed to be. As for the hens, they can go anywhere. The farmer said so. Don't be

unkind, or you will make no friends. Didn't your mother tell you that?'

Snowball suddenly thought of his mother. Yes, she *had* told him that. Oh dear – and he had forgotten so soon. What a pity! He hung his head down and trotted off to a corner. The hens came round and clucked at him.

'He's only a baby after all! He doesn't know any better. What's your name, baby?'

The pony felt glad he had a name. 'My name is Snowball,' he said.

Then the hens and the brown horse laughed loudly. 'What a joke!' they said to one another. 'Snowball! Think of that! What a black Snowball!'

The gate clicked and the pony heard the voices of the children. He pricked up his ears and looked round.

'Snowball! Snowball!' called the three children. The little pony galloped gladly over to them.

'He knows his name already!' cried Willie. 'Isn't he clever? He came as soon as he was called.'

The pony nuzzled against them. Timmy held something out to him, something square and white on the palm of his hand.

Snowball sniffed at it.

'Go on, Snowball, it's a treat for you. It's a piece of sugar,' said Timmy. 'Eat it, silly!'

Snowball sniffed again. He had never smelt sugar before. He suddenly lifted his upper lip and took the sugar lump into his mouth.

He crunched it. It was sweet and he liked it very much. He sniffed round Timmy hoping to find another bit of sugar. What a nice boy this was, to give him such a treat!

'I may bring you a lump of sugar tomorrow, if you're good,' said Sheila. 'Come

31

along. Let's see you gallop and trot and walk and roll. We've come to play with you for the whole afternoon!'

Soon the four of them were playing madly together, with all the hens looking on in surprise. The children galloped round the field and the pony galloped too. They walked and he walked. They lay down on the grass and he lay down too.

Then they rolled over and over and the pony rolled over as well. That was a game he liked! The children laughed.

'He's just like us!' said Timmy. 'He likes just the same things as we do!'

Chapter 4
Snowball and Sheila

The first night Snowball felt dreadfully lonely without his mother to snuggle up against. Usually she lay down beneath a big chestnut tree in her field, and the little pony cuddled close up to her.

But tonight, in his own field, there was no one to cuddle against. He neighed for his mother, but she didn't come. She was far away. He looked for the brown hens to talk to, but they had gone to bed in the hen-house.

He went to the hedge and neighed for the old brown horse. But the horse was asleep at the other end of the field and didn't come.

An owl came out and screeched suddenly. It made Snowball jump.

Then a hedgehog ran by, and scraped

33

against his hooves.

And then the moon rose up, a big round lamp in the sky, that seemed like a face to Snowball.

He was lonely and afraid. He stood under a tree and trembled. He was very unhappy. Nobody loved him. Everyone had forgotten about him! He wanted to run away, but the field-gate was shut.

But somebody remembered him. Somebody lay still in her warm bed, and thought of the little pony out in the field alone for the first time in his life. Somebody was sad for him, and wanted to comfort him.

That somebody was Sheila. Sheila loved her dolls and all her toys, and now she loved the pony.

She got up and went to the window. The moon was up and she could see the pony's field.

Then she saw him, standing up, quite still, in one corner. 'He's awake! He can't go to sleep. He wants his mother!' thought the little girl. 'Poor little Snowball. I'll pull on my dressing-gown and steal downstairs and run to the field. It's such a fine night I shan't get cold.'

She put on her dressing-gown, and crept down the stairs. She undid the front door and slipped out. She ran down the garden path to the white gate. Then she went to the field and opened the gate there.

Snowball heard the click and was alarmed. Who was this? Who could it be in the middle of the night? His mother had always told him that people who crept about at night-time were not good people. Had someone come to steal him?

He stood and shivered, as Sheila came through the gate. Then he heard a soft voice, 'Poor little Snowball! Are you lonely? I've just come to tell you not to be unhappy, and to give you a hug.'

Snowball knew Sheila's voice. His heart jumped for joy. He trotted over to her at once, nuzzling against her, almost knocking her over. He was delighted to see someone he knew. She put her arms round him, and he felt her heart beating against his nose. Nice girl! He would love her the best because she was so kind.

'Now you lie down here, under this tree where the ground is dry,' said Sheila, and she led him to a good place. 'You'll soon be asleep. Nothing will harm you here.'

Snowball took hold of her dressing-gown gently with his teeth. He pulled at it.

'What, you want me to lie down near you!' said Sheila. 'What a funny little pony you are! Do you miss your mother tonight! Well, I'll cuddle up to you for a little while, then I must go in.'

It was a very warm night. Snowball and

Sheila lay down on the dry grass, and Sheila put her head on the pony's round body. He was quite happy now. Somebody loved him, and was his friend. That was what his mother had said – he must get friends and he would be happy.

He fell asleep – and so did Sheila! The round moon looked down on them both. A hedgehog came up and stared at them in surprise.

They both slept for hours. Then Dan, the farm-hand, came into the field – and how surprised he was to see Sheila and Snowball asleep together under the tree!

'Hi, Missy!' he said, gently, and shook her shoulder. 'You'll get into trouble for sleeping out of doors. You might get a dreadful cold!'

Sheila woke up and stared into the green leaves of the tree above her. She saw the blue sky between some of the leaves.

Wherever could she be?

She sat up and saw Dan. 'Oh dear!' she said. 'I must have been out here all night! Whatever will Mother say? She will be very cross with me. I wonder if I can slip into the house without being seen.'

'No, don't you do that,' said Dan. 'You tell your mother, see? It doesn't do to hide things, that's not right. My, that's a fine little black pony, isn't it? What's his name?'

'Snowball,' said Sheila, and that made Dan laugh.

'What a joke!' he said. He stroked Snowball, and the pony pushed his nose against him. He nuzzled against Sheila too. He thought he would never, never forget how the little girl had come out to him on the night when he was so lonely. He would love Sheila best.

The little girl ran indoors. Her mother saw

her coming and was surprised. 'Surely you haven't been out in the fields in your dressing-gown!' she said.

'Oh Mother, I've been out all night, quite by mistake!' said Sheila. 'Snowball was so lonely, and I knew he was missing his mother. So I went out to him, and we cuddled up together. And I fell asleep and Dan woke me up. Don't be cross with me!'

Mother wasn't. She gave Sheila a kiss and said, 'You're always such a kind little girl, aren't you!'

After that, Sheila and Snowball were always special friends.

Chapter 5
Snowball Makes a
Few Friends

Snowball soon settled down in his new home. He loved all the children. One or other of them always brought him a lump of sugar, and he looked forward to that.

Soon he was allowed to go wherever he wanted to. His gate was not always shut, and he wandered in and out as he liked. He was as much a pet as Tinker, the farm-dog.

Snowball liked his new home. He soon began to know all the other animals on the farm. He went round to tell them who he was.

He went into the field where the cows were. They stared at him, munching all the time. He looked at their horns and felt a little afraid.

'You won't toss me, will you?' he said. 'Promise you won't.'

'Of course not. We don't use our horns for tossing,' said Buttercup, a red and white cow. 'The *bull* might use his horns to toss you, though, so don't go near him.'

'I'm Snowball, the new Shetland pony, and I belong to the children,' said Snowball. The cows laughed.

'Snowball! What an odd name for you! We have never seen a horse as tiny as you are. We thought you were a toy one at first.'

'I'm not a toy! I'm alive!' said Snowball. 'See how fast I can gallop!'

He galloped round and round the field and the cows watched him. 'You gallop almost as fast as Captain, the big brown horse over there,' said Buttercup.

Snowball ran up to Captain. 'Hello!' he said. 'I'm Snowball, the Shetland pony. I can gallop faster than you, I'm sure.'

'Ah, you're the fellow who played "catch" with the hens and couldn't catch them, aren't you?' said Captain, with a twinkle in his eye. 'Well, I'll run a race with you if you like.'

So they ran a race round and round the

field, but Captain won. He was a strong and powerful horse, and though Snowball galloped as fast as he could, he couldn't keep up with Captain.

'I can't gallop as fast as you can, after all,' said Snowball, panting.

'No. It's better not to boast of what you can do, till you've tried,' said Captain. 'Now, where are you off to?'

'I'm going to talk to those round pink creatures over there,' said Snowball. 'What are they? They make such a funny grunting noise.'

'Pigs,' said Captain. 'Now, don't you go into their sty, because if you do the old sow may come after you. She doesn't like people she doesn't know.'

But Snowball took no notice. He trotted off to the pigsty. He pushed against the gate. It didn't open. Then he remembered seeing one of the children press down the catch at one side of the gate. That made the gate open.

So with his nose he pressed on the catch. It opened. Aha, how clever he was! He trotted into the pigsty, and all the piglets ran round him in wonder.

'What are you? Who are you?'

'I'm Snowball, the Shetland pony, and I am allowed to go where I like,' said Snowball. 'Ah, what's in your trough? It smells good!'

He went over to the pig-trough, in which Dan had put pig-food. He began to nibble bits here and there.

The old mother sow, who had been lying down on her side, lifted her head and looked at him.

'What are you doing in here, eating our food?' she grunted. 'Go out at once. And shut the gate behind you. I don't want my piglets running all over the farm.'

Snowball ran to the gate and shut it. But he didn't go out of it first! No, he shut himself in, and went back to the trough to find another titbit.

The big old sow was angry. She stood herself up on her four short legs and looked crossly at Snowball out of her little piggy eyes.

'Bad pony!' she said. 'Stealing our food, and opening our gate! Bad pony!'

She ran at Snowball and almost knocked him over. He was frightened. She looked so very long and fat and big.

The piglets ran round him, squealing, 'Run away, silly, run away!'

So he ran round the pigsty with the old mother-pig lumbering after him. The piglets ran too, squealing in excitement, getting under his feet. Oh dear, why had he come into this horrid place?

Willie heard all the noise. He ran to the pigsty, and how he laughed.

'Mother, look! Sheila, look! Snowball has got in among the pigs, and the old sow is chasing him!'

Everyone laughed and Snowball was ashamed. Willie opened the pigsty and Snowball rushed out. The pigs put their pink noses through the lowest bars of the gate and squealed again.

'Come and see us again, Snowball. It's fun to see Mother chasing you!'

'Did you open the gate yourself?' said Willie to Snowball, astonished. 'My goodness, what a clever pony you are! But don't you go into the pigsty again. The old sow doesn't like it.'

'I won't,' neighed Snowball, and trotted back to his own field for a rest. 'Dear me,

how glad I am that I didn't have a fierce
mother like that old sow! I am sorry for all
those piglets!'

Chapter 6
A Saddle and Bridle for Snowball

The first time that Snowball had on a saddle and bridle he didn't like it at all. He couldn't understand what was on his back. He didn't like the bridle either, and he tossed his head up and down angrily.

'Now, don't be silly, Snowball,' said Sheila, in her gentle voice. 'We all want to ride you, and we can't if you don't have a saddle for us to sit on, and reins to guide you.'

She gave him a lump of sugar. He munched it and stood quietly. He looked at her out of the corners of his eyes. If Sheila wanted him to do something, he would do it. Yes, he would do anything for Sheila, even if he didn't like it.

'You get on first, Sheila,' said Willie. 'The pony loves you so much, ever since that night you spent with him in the field. He may stand quietly for you.'

So Sheila got on to his back. How heavy she felt at first. How uncomfortable! Snowball wanted to rear up and throw off this sudden weight.

But he couldn't bear to make Sheila fall off. She might be hurt. So he stood still, trembling.

'Dear Snowball, dear good Snowball,' said Sheila, and she stroked his thick black mane.

'Walk with me on your back, Snowball. You and I are one, now, can't you feel how we belong to one another, now that you carry me on your back? Our Daddy says that that is one of the nicest feelings between a man and a horse. Can't you feel it, Snowball?'

She pressed her legs against his sides. He

stopped trembling. He walked a few steps. He suddenly liked Sheila being on his back. He stopped and looked round at her. She patted him.

'Good boy,' she said. 'Clever boy! You will soon be as good to ride as Captain, the old brown horse.'

'I'm better than Captain for you, because I am the right size!' neighed Snowball, and he suddenly set off round the field, with Sheila holding the reins in delight. Bumpity-bumpity-bump! Bumpity-bumpity-bump! she went.

'Steady, Snowball, steady, you're bumping me so!' cried Sheila. 'This is your first lesson so you must only walk with me.'

So Snowball walked and jogged round the field with Sheila on his back. Sheila laughed for joy, and her cheeks went bright red. Her eyes shone.

'He's lovely to ride!' she called. 'Simply lovely. He will go like the wind! Whoa, Snowball. Whoa! When I pull the reins in like this, you must stop. That's right.'

Timmy had a ride next. He wasn't so good at riding as Sheila was, for she had often ridden before. So Willie went beside them, his hands on the reins.

Then Willie had his turn and he walked and trotted round the field. The noise of Snowball's little hooves made all the brown hens scuttle away into the hedge.

Snowball felt proud when at last Willie dismounted. He had taken three children for rides. He had got used to a saddle almost at once. He knew how to answer the pull of the reins.

'He's really very clever,' said Willie, and he patted Snowball's velvety nose. 'He'll do anything for us. He was frightened at first, but he soon got over it. Isn't he lovely to ride, Sheila?'

'Yes, lovely,' said Sheila. 'He's just the right size for us. Even if Timmy fell off his back it wouldn't matter, because he wouldn't have far to fall! Good boy, Snowball. We'll take you over to see your mother tomorrow, if you like, and show her how well you've got on. That shall be your reward for being so good.'

Snowball galloped round the field all by himself in delight. To see his mother! Oh, how lovely! And she would see how well he carried the children on his back, and he could tell her about the pigs and cows and everything.

So the next day the four of them, with

Tinker the farm-dog, started off to the near-by farm. Mother had said that as it was such a fine day they could take their lunch with them and have it in the fields.

They saddled Snowball. Then they set off, taking it in turns to ride on his back. He felt very proud, because everyone they met stared hard. Boys and girls ran up to them and patted Snowball. 'Oh, is he yours? Isn't he a beauty? What's his name?'

'Snowball,' said Willie, and the children laughed.

'What a funny name for a black pony! Can we have a ride?'

'Not today,' said Willie. 'He's only just learnt to have us on his back. We're taking him to see his mother.'

'Let me have a ride on him, do,' said a big boy, tugging at the reins.

'Let go,' said Willie. 'No, Lennie, you can't. You're too big, for one thing, and for another you're not kind to animals. Let go!'

'Well, I shall come and get him to ride one day when you're all out!' said Lennie, looking sulky. 'See? That's what I'll do if you don't give me a ride now.'

'Don't be silly,' said Willie. 'Come on, Sheila, you get on Snowball's back now. It's your turn.'

Sheila got up, and they went off again. Tinker followed them, looking round and growling at Lennie. Nobody liked Lennie. He was selfish and unkind.

'Here we are!' said Willie at last, as they came in sight of the farm. 'There's your old field, Snowball.'

'And there's my mother!' whinnied Snowball, in delight. 'Look, there she is!'

Chapter 7
A Visit to
Snowball's Mother

With Sheila on his back the little pony trotted to the gate of the field he knew so well. He whinnied loudly. His mother lifted her head and saw him at the gate.

She galloped over at once, whinnying too. She and Snowball rubbed noses lovingly.

'We'll have our picnic in this field,' said Willie. 'Then Snowball and his mother can have a nice long time together.'

Sheila got off Snowball's back, took his saddle and bridle off and led him through the gate, which Willie had opened. The children followed and shut the gate. They found a nice place on a sunny bank and sat down to eat their lunch.

'Look at Snowball and his mother,' said Timmy. 'Aren't they pleased to see one another?'

Snowball looked round the field. He remembered how it had seemed enormous to him, like half the world. Now it looked very small! How strange. Had he grown, or had the field got small?

His mother looked smaller to him too. So he must have grown. His mother told him he had got bigger.

'You're almost as big as I am!' she said. 'How quickly you've grown! Have you got a name yet?'

'Yes. It's Snowball,' said the pony. His mother thought that was funny.

'Why is it funny?' asked Snowball. 'Everyone laughs at my name. Why do they?'

'Wait till next winter comes and you will know why,' said his mother. 'Now, tell me everything about your new home. Are the children nice?'

Snowball told her everything. He told her about how Sheila had come to comfort him on his first lonely night, and his mother was glad.

'She must be a dear little girl,' she said. 'I will let her ride me after she has had her lunch.'

'They're all nice,' said Snowball. 'Except the old sow, who looks after the piglets. She chased me.'

'Look, the children are calling us. They have got some oats,' said his mother. So they cantered over to the children.

When they had finished the oats, Sheila held out a young carrot for Snowball's mother, who took it eagerly. She loved carrots.

Snowball sniffed at it.

'Try one, Snowball,' said Willie. 'You'll like it.'

Snowball liked it very much and nosed in the lunch-bag for another. He found one and took it out.

'Oh look – Snowball is helping himself!' cried Sheila. 'No, Snowball, don't you take those apples! They're for us!'

But Sheila gave Snowball the apple cores and he crunched them up, pleased. Then he went round the old field with his mother, looking for the places he knew. Yes, there was the tree they used to sleep under. And there was the ditch where the long juicy grass grew. And there was the trough in which the farmer always put water, because there was no stream or pond in the field.

Soon the children got up and went over to the ponies. Snowball's mother tried to show Sheila that she would like to give her a ride. But she had no saddle.

'I think I could ride her bareback if she would let me hold her mane,' said Sheila, and got up on to the pony's back. Soon she was trotting round the field, and Timmy followed her on Snowball. Willie stood in the middle, waving a long twig about, pretending he was a circus ringmaster, and they were his circus ponies and riders!

'It's time to go home,' said Sheila at last, getting off the mother pony's back. 'Thank you, I loved that ride. Snowball, say goodbye

to your mother.'

'You won't be lonely again without me, will you?' said Snowball's mother, nuzzling against him. 'Do you want to stay here with me? Are you sad to go away?'

'No,' said Snowball. 'I love my new home, and I love the three children. I don't want to stay here, Mother. But I'll come and see you again soon, even if I have to come by myself. Goodbye!'

'Goodbye, Snowball!'

He walked away, with Timmy on his back, a sleek and shining pony. His mother watched him go, very proud of him. The gate clicked.

They were gone.

Chapter 8
Snowball Is Funny

Once, when the three children were all indoors, because it was pouring with rain, Snowball felt wet and cold and lonely.

He stood under a tree, but the rain was coming down so hard that he got wet even there. He whinnied crossly.

'I'm getting wet. I shall get a cold. My mother always told me not to get a chill. Even the hens are safely in their house – but I am left out in this field all by myself!'

He heard some ducks splashing in a big puddle on the other side of the hedge. He looked over and spoke to them.

'Fancy being out in the rain! How stupid you are! You will get wet through.'

'Ah, this is proper duck's weather,'

quacked a big drake. 'We love the rain. The wetter it is the more we like it. Our bodies never get wet. The rain slips off our feathers, you know.'

'The pigs are in their sty, the cat is in the house, the hens are underneath their wooden hut, the dog is in his kennel – but I am here getting wetter and wetter and wetter!' whinnied Snowball, feeling more and more sorry for himself.

'Well, go and ask the hens if you can shelter in their house,' said the ducks, splashing

hard. 'There is plenty of room there.'

So Snowball cantered to the gate of his field. It was shut, but he knew how to open any field-gate, clever little pony! Soon the gate was open and he trotted over to the big hen-house.

But the hens did not want him in there. 'No, no, you chased us out of your field the other day,' they said. 'We don't want you in our house.'

Then Snowball went to the kitchen door and looked in to see if the cat was there. She was lying on the mat by the kitchen fire.

'Can I come in and lie down by the fire too?' said Snowball.

'Good gracious, no!' said the cat. 'Only dogs and cats are allowed indoors. Go away.'

But Snowball went right into the kitchen, and was just going to lie down by the fire when the daily help came in. 'My goodness!' she cried in astonishment, 'Whatever next! Snowball, go out at once! Stamping all over the kitchen! Do you want to be smacked?'

Then Snowball went to Tinker's kennel. Tinker wasn't there. The kennel was made of an enormous old tub set on its side.

Inside was some straw. It looked very, very comfortable.

'This looks good,' thought Snowball. 'I'm so small, and the tub is so big, I believe I could get into it and lie down.'

So into the tub he got, pushing himself in backwards very carefully. He lay down in the straw. It was dry and soft and comfortable. Snowball was happy.

'I wish I was a dog. I wish I had a kennel like this. Tinker is very lucky,' he said to himself. And then he fell asleep.

The rain stopped. The sun came out. The children came out, too, and looked for Snowball, because they wanted to ride him.

'He's not in his field!' said Sheila, surprised. 'He's opened the gate and gone. Snowball! Where are you?'

There was no answer. Then suddenly, from the yard, came the sound of loud barking. It was Tinker.

'Whatever's the matter with Tinker?' said Timmy.

Tinker was standing outside his kennel, barking loudly. And there, inside, just waking up, was Snowball, looking very surprised.

'*Snowball!* Oh! do look, Snowball's put

himself in Tinker's kennel!' cried Willie, and
how they all laughed.

Snowball scrambled out and shook himself. He neighed and trotted up to Sheila.
He was glad to see her, and he put his nose
into her hand.

'You're a funny darling pony!' said Sheila,
and she laughed at him. 'I'm sure no other
pony in all the world has slept in a dog's kennel, Snowball. Whatever will you think of
next?'

Chapter 9
The Bad Boy, Lennie

Once Lennie came to see Willie, Sheila and Timmy. They didn't much want to see him, because they didn't like him. He was very unkind and selfish.

But Mother had always said they must be polite to visitors, so they were quite nice to him.

'I want to ride that pony of yours,' said Lennie.

'No, we'd rather you didn't,' said Sheila, very politely. 'He's still rather new, and although he's used to us, he might not like you riding him. You see, you are very fat and heavy.'

'Don't be rude,' said Lennie, frowning. He *was* very fat, because he was a greedy boy, but

66

he didn't like being reminded of it, of course.

'I'm not being rude,' said Sheila, surprised. 'I'm just telling you why you can't ride Snowball.'

'Well, I'm going to,' said Lennie, who knew that the children's father and mother were out. He went over to Snowball's field. The children ran after him.

'You're not to, Lennie,' said Willie.

'You can't stop me,' said Lennie. 'I'm much bigger than you are. I could knock you all down with one hand.'

'You're a very horrid boy,' said Sheila, almost in tears.

Timmy caught hold of Lennie's coat and tried to drag him back. Lennie shook himself free and Timmy fell over.

Then Lennie ran fast to the field, climbed the gate and called to Snowball. 'Snowball, come here!'

'No, don't come, don't come!' cried Sheila.

But Snowball did come. He always came when he was called. He came now, trotting up, his bright eyes looking from one child to another, ready to give any of them a ride.

But it was Lennie who jumped on his back. Lennie had no saddle or bridle for the pony, but he didn't care. He held on to Snowball's thick black mane, and clasped him tightly with his strong knees.

'Gallop!' cried Lennie. 'Go on, gallop!'

Snowball didn't like this boy. He was fat and heavy, and he didn't feel nice. Lennie kicked hard against the pony's sides, and Snowball jumped in fright. He wasn't used to people being rough with him.

'Oh Lennie, don't! Oh Lennie, get off!' cried Sheila, running after them. But now Snowball was galloping in alarm over the field, bucking as he went, afraid of Lennie's hard heels.

'Here we go, here we go!' cried Lennie, enjoying himself. 'Go on, Snowball, faster, faster!'

Snowball didn't like this boy on his back. He was a horrid boy. The little pony suddenly stopped dead, and Lennie shot right over his head, and landed with a bump on the grass.

All the three children laughed. It served Lennie right. But Lennie was very angry indeed. He went to the hedge and cut a thick stick with his knife, holding on to Snowball all the time.

Then he jumped on to the pony's back again and began to hit him hard with the stick.

'I'll teach you to throw me over your head, you wicked pony!' he cried. The three children rushed up to stop him, but Lennie made Snowball gallop away from them.

Nobody knew what to do. Lennie was such a big boy. But Snowball knew what to do.

He wasn't going to put up with that boy one minute longer!

He galloped to the open gate. He galloped right through it. He galloped to the pond where the ducks were swimming lazily.

He galloped right to the very edge – and then, just as suddenly as before, he stopped – and over his head again went Lennie, straight into the muddy duck-pond!

The ducks fled in fright, quacking loudly. Snowball raised his head and neighed in delight. Sheila, Willie and Timmy roared with laughter. Lennie had got a very good punishment indeed.

The surprised boy went head-over-heels into the water. He struggled to his feet,

choking and spluttering, angry and frightened. He waded out, weeds hanging from his hair, his clothes dripping wet.

'What will my mother say?' he said, and, to Willie's astonishment, he began to howl loudly.

'Baby!' said Willie. 'You are bully enough to kick and whip a little pony, and baby enough to howl when you're punished! Go home. I won't tell my father about you this time, because Snowball himself has punished you.'

Lennie went home, still howling. Snowball stood with the three children, neighing.

'You're the cleverest pony I ever knew!' said Timmy, hugging him. 'We needn't worry about you, ever, because you always find a way out of any difficulty. Good little Snowball! Come and have a special lump of sugar.'

Chapter 10
Snowball Uses His Brains

Every week Willie rode on Snowball's back to the village, to fetch the papers for his father. There were five weekly papers; three for his father and two for his mother.

Snowball soon knew when Friday came. He didn't wait for Willie to come and fetch him. He opened the gate with his nose, and trotted down to the garden-door of the house. He knew Willie would come rushing out in a minute or two.

'Hello, Snowball!' Willie would shout. 'Always on time, aren't you! Come on, we'll go and get the papers. I've got the money.'

But one day, when Snowball went down to the garden-door and waited patiently, no

Willie came. Snowball stamped his feet and neighed. That meant 'Willie, come along,

you *are* late!'

But still no Willie came. Then the daily help shouted from the kitchen: 'My, there's Snowball waiting for Willie to fetch the papers as usual! He doesn't know Willie's in bed with a cold!'

Snowball pricked up his ears. What, Willie in bed! Oh, that was why he hadn't seen him all day, then.

Poor Willie!

Snowball trotted off. He stood in the lane, thinking. He knew the way to the village. He knew the paper shop. Why shouldn't he go by himself? The woman at the shop would know what he had come for.

The clever little pony set off by himself, tossing his head and whisking his long tail proudly. He was going to fetch the papers. He felt most important.

'I'm fetching the papers,' he told all the dogs he met.

'I'm fetching the papers,' he told the old cart-horses he passed. Everyone stared at him in wonder.

He came to the village. 'Oh look, there's

Willie's dear little Shetland pony out by himself!' cried all the children, and Snowball whinnied to them too.

'I'm fetching the papers!'

He came to the paper shop. There was a bell-pull that hung outside the door. Snowball would have gone into the shop if the door had been open, but it wasn't. He had often seen Willie pull the bell, so he reached up to it with his mouth, took hold of the rope, and dragged it down.

'Ring-ting-ting!' the bell jangled loudly. Then Snowball knocked with his hoof on the ground. 'Knock, knock, knock,' just as he did when Willie was on his back, waiting to get the papers.

The shop-woman opened the shop door and looked out, expecting to see Willie. But only Snowball was there, and she stared in surprise.

'Why, where's Willie?' she said. 'Have you come without him?'

Snowball saw some papers hanging up in a rack just inside the shop. He tried to get them with his mouth.

The woman laughed.

'No, no, not those! Those aren't the right

ones. Have you come for the papers all by yourself? Wait a minute and I'll get them for you.'

She went inside the shop. Snowball mounted the two steps up to the shop, pushed open the door and walked inside. The woman laughed again as she wrapped up the five papers in brown paper and string.

'I never knew such a pony, never! Coming for the papers on the right day, and walking into my shop, after ringing the bell and all!

You ought to be in a circus!'

Snowball had no money, so he couldn't pay. He took the roll of papers in his mouth and stamped out of the shop. He galloped all the way back to the farm.

He saw Willie's father in the field nearby and ran up to him. He dropped the papers at his feet.

'Bless us all!' cried the farmer, in astonishment and delight. 'Don't tell me you've fetched the papers all by yourself! Snowball, you're a wonder, you really are! Thank you, little pony, you're a good little fellow, and I'll give you four of my best carrots as a reward!'

And he did!

Chapter 11
Snowball at the Garden Party

One day Mother had a letter and she read it out to the children. 'It's from Lady Tomms,' she said. 'She's going to hold a big garden party in her grounds, and there will be all kinds of side-shows to make money to go towards the hospital.'

'Are we going?' said the children, eagerly.

'Well, Lady Tomms wonders if you would like to organise some races, Willie – and Sheila, she thought perhaps you could make

78

some little flower button-holes and sell them.'

'Mother, I don't want to organise races,' said Willie.

'And when I sold buttonholes before, hardly anyone bought them,' said Sheila.

'Well – I'd like you to do *something* to help!' said Mother.

Timmy had a sudden idea. 'Mother! I know what we could do! We could take Snowball and charge children ten pence a ride!'

'That's a very good idea,' said Mother.

'I could plait a red ribbon in his mane, and brush his tail out beautifully,' said Sheila. 'Oh Mother, wouldn't everyone love Snowball?'

So it was decided that Snowball should be taken along to the garden party, and should give rides to the children there. Mother thought they ought to charge twenty pence, not ten pence.

The children told Dan about it, and he had a fine idea. 'I believe I could make you a little pony-cart, a very small one, just big enough for Snowball to draw,' he said.

Dan kept his word. He made a most beautiful little cart, with two big wheels, which he painted red, with yellow spokes. He painted the cart red too, with a yellow line running round it, and made a set of harness from some old leather straps for Snowball.

'Perhaps Snowball won't like it,' said Sheila. But he did. He felt very grown-up and important to have a cart of his own.

He looked simply lovely trotting along with the little cart behind him. Timmy often rode in it, and he said it was almost as nice as riding on Snowball's back.

The day of the garden party came. Sheila had bought some dark red ribbon, and she carefully plaited it in and out of Snowball's thick black mane. Then she brushed his tail out beautifully.

They put Snowball into the shafts of the little cart that Dan had made, and set off to Lady Tomms' big garden. They found Lady Tomms and she showed them where they were to take children for rides, up and down the big drive.

'How lovely your pony looks!' she said. 'I always do like Shetland ponies, but I think yours is the very nicest that I've ever seen.'

There were all kinds of side-shows and

races and competitions.

But the favourite side-show of all was Snowball!

First Willie called out loudly, 'Rides on Snowball, twenty pence a time! Rides on Snowball, twenty pence a time!'

Then Sheila lined up the children, waiting for their turn. Timmy took their money and put it proudly into a big red bag. Then Willie helped each child on in his turn and took them trotting up and down the drive.

Soon Sheila brought out the red and yellow cart, and Willie called out loudly, 'Rides for the tiny ones, ten pence each. Only ten pence a ride in this lovely little cart!'

Then the very tiny children were lined up with their mothers, waiting their turn. Timmy took their money. Their mothers lifted them into the little cart behind Snowball, and Willie led the pony up and down the drive. The tiny children were delighted.

How hard the three children and Snowball worked all that afternoon! Three times Timmy's bag was full and he had to go to Lady Tomms and empty it. You will never guess how much money he had at the end of the afternoon!

'My dears, do you know you have made twenty-five pounds and ten pence out of pony-rides?' said Lady Tomms, in surprise. 'More than any other side-show has made. It is simply wonderful.'

Willie, Sheila and Timmy were so pleased. Sheila hugged Snowball and whispered into his ear, 'I'm so proud of you, Snowball.'

Wouldn't you love to ride on Snowball? Well, if you ever see a dear little black Shetland pony, call out Snowball! Snowball!

If he comes running to you and nuzzles his nose into your hand, you'll know what he wants to say. 'I like you! You can have a ride on my back!'

Bimbo and Topsy

Bimbo and Topsy

Enid Blyton
Illustrations by Guy Parker-Rees

BLOOMSBURY
CHILDREN'S
BOOKS

Contents

A letter from Bimbo

Hello, children!

I do think it's fun to have a book of my own, don't you? I've been looking through the pages, and I think I look very nice in the pictures. If you colour me with your crayons, don't forget to give me blue eyes, not green.

I do a lot of naughty things in this book – but Mistress says she wouldn't part with me, even if I were twice as bad. So she must love me very much, mustn't she? I hope you will love me too, when you read my book. I am sharing it with Topsy, the puppy. She will write you a letter at the end.

A hundred purrs from,

Bimbo

Chapter 1
The New Little Kitten

One day a little kitten arrived in a basket at a house called Green Hedges.
He was a present for two little girls there,
and how they squealed with joy to see him!

'He's not a bit like an ordinary cat!' said
Gillian. 'He's creamy-white, and he's got a
chocolate-brown nose, ears, feet and tail!'

'And do look at his eyes!' said Imogen.
'They are bright blue – like the sea on a summer's day.'

So they were. The kitten looked up at the
two little girls with his brilliant eyes, and
then jumped out of the basket.

'Mee-ow-ee-ow!' he said. 'Of course I'm
not like an ordinary cat – I'm a Siamese cat,
didn't you know? We are always brown and

cream, and our eyes are always blue! I've
come to live with you.'

He jumped up on to Gillian's lap. 'I
haven't a name,' he mewed. 'You must give
me one. How can I come when I'm called if I
haven't a name?'

'We can't call you, silly, if you haven't a
name!' said Gillian. 'Imogen – what shall we
call him?'

'Paddy-paws,' said Imogen.

'No – that's too long,' said Gillian. 'What

about Whiskers?'

'All the cats in the garden would come if we called "Whiskers, Whiskers!"' said Imogen, 'because they've all got whiskers.'

'Well – let's call him *Bimbo* then!' said Gillian. 'Mummy once had a cat she loved called Bimbo – and this is a cat we shall love, so we'll call him Bimbo.'

'That's a nice name,' said Imogen. 'I shall like calling that. I shall often stand in the garden and call Bim-bim-bim-bimbo!'

'Do you like that name, Bimbo?' said Gillian, and she stroked the creamy coat of the new kitten. He nibbled at her fingers!

'Mee-ow! Yes – that's a nice name for a cat like me. I'm glad I've got a name. Now I feel real. You don't feel real if you haven't a name. Let me go into the corner over there and hide. Then you call me, and I'll come. I shall feel a proper cat then.'

He jumped off Gillian's knee and ran to the corner. He hid under a chair and waited. The two children called him loudly.

'Bim-bim-bimbo! Bim-bim-bimbo!'

'Mee-ow!' said Bimbo, and sprang out of the corner at once. 'I'm here! I'm Bimbo!'

And that is how Bimbo came to the nursery and got his name. He soon settled down there and grew to know everyone in the house.

There was Bobs, the big black-and-white fox-terrier, a kindly old dog who didn't seem to mind if Bimbo jumped out to frighten him. There was Cosy, a fat tabby, two years old, who smacked Bimbo when he was rude to her. There were the white pigeons in the garden, that Gillian said Bimbo was never to touch. And there were the grey doves in the big cage, who said 'Coo-coo-coo' all day long.

Bobs went out for walks with the children. Bimbo wanted to go too. But Gillian said no.

'You would be frightened of the cars,' she said, 'and the dogs would chase you.'

'Oh no, they wouldn't,' said Bimbo. 'Bobs doesn't chase me – and he's a dog, isn't he? As for cars, I don't even know what they are. But I'm sure I wouldn't be afraid of them, if you don't mind them, Gillian!'

'No, you mustn't come,' said the children, and they went off out of the front gate with Bobs trotting beside them.

'I *will* go!' thought Bimbo, and he ran to the hedge that grew round the front garden.

'I'm not afraid of dogs or of cars either! I'll join the children and Bobs when they come by – and how surprised they will be to see me trotting with them too!'

So when Bobs and the children came by on the pavement near the hedge, Bimbo crept out and ran behind them. Pad-pad-pad, his feet went, pad-pad-pad. Bobs turned round and looked at him.

'You naughty kitten!' said Bobs. 'You heard what the children said. Go home.'

'I shan't,' said Bimbo. 'I want to go for a walk just as you do. I'm a big kitten now.'

Just then a car raced by and Bimbo meowed in fright. 'Oh, what's that enormous thing? Oh, it's shouting at me. I don't like it! Bobs, Bobs, will it eat me?'

'Bimbo, that's only a car hooting,' said Bobs. 'Of course it won't eat you.'

'There's another one!' cried Bimbo. 'Oh, suppose it comes on the pavement and gobbles me up? Bobs, I know those big things would eat me for their dinner.'

'No, they wouldn't,' said Bobs. 'They don't have any dinner. Don't be silly.'

Suddenly a dog came by, and was most surprised to see a kitten out for a walk. 'Wuff!'

he barked. 'Look what's here to chase! Run, kitten, run, I'm going to come after you!'

'You're not to!' mewed Bimbo, and ran between Bobs' legs. 'Save me, Bobs, save me!'

'You're tripping me up!' cried Bobs. And down he went on to the pavement with a bump. The children looked round to see what the matter was – and how surprised they were to see naughty Bimbo tearing down the pavement as fast as his brown legs would take him – with a dog after him, barking madly!

'Where's the gate, oh, where's the gate?' panted Bimbo. 'I can't see it! I've passed it! I must climb a tree!'

So up a tree went the kitten, and was very glad that the dog couldn't climb it too. The dog sat down at the foot, his tongue hanging out.

'I'll wait till you come down,' he said. 'You're good to chase!'

So there poor Bimbo had to stay till the children came back from their walk and saw him.

'Oh, look! There's poor Bimbo up the tree!' said Gillian in surprise. 'Go away, dog!

Bimbo, jump on to my shoulder!'

So down Bimbo jumped and landed safely on Gillian's shoulder. The dog ran away.

'I'll watch for you to go walking again,' he wuffed. 'Then we'll have another race!'

But Bimbo had had enough of going for walks! '*You* can go out each day for a walk, Bobs,' he said, 'and so can Gillian and Imogen. But I shan't. Walks are dangerous for kittens like me!'

'Well, isn't that exactly what I told you?' wuffed Bobs. 'You just be sensible – or I'll chase you myself!'

Chapter 2
A Playmate for Bimbo

Bimbo wanted somebody to play with. Bobs didn't always want to play. Cosy didn't mind sometimes, but if Bimbo was rough, she smacked him hard with her paw and he didn't like that.

Gillian and Imogen went to school. So there wasn't really anyone for him to play with.

'I wish I had someone to play with!' he kept sighing. 'I do wish I had. Somebody silly like myself, who will play chase-my-tail and hide-under-the-bed, and skip-around, and pounce-at-your-feet. Those are the games I love. But nobody will play them with me.'

And then one day a playmate came for Bimbo. She came in a big basket, much bigger than the one Bimbo had come in. She arrived at the station in this basket, and she was fetched in the car. The basket was put down in the nursery, and the two children looked at it excitedly.

'Somebody nice is in here,' said Mummy, and she undid the strap.

'Who?' asked Gillian. 'Do tell us! Is it somebody for us?'

'Yes, for you,' said Mummy. 'Somebody to live in the nursery and belong to you. It's a little puppy called Topsy!'

Up went the lid – but nobody jumped out. The children and Mummy looked inside. There, on some straw, lay a small white fox-terrier dog, with a pretty black head and black tail. She looked up at the three people with soft brown eyes. She was frightened.

'Hello, Topsy!' said Gillian, in a gentle voice. 'Don't be frightened! You've come to a good home, and we will love you and be kind to you. Jump out and let us have a look at you.'

Topsy stood up. She was a dear little puppy about five months old. She wagged her tail just a little. It was a signal to say that she wanted to be friends.

'You poor little frightened thing!' said Imogen. 'I expect you can't understand being sent away from your mother and your home. This must seem very strange to you. Never mind – you will soon know us and get used to us. We will love you very much, and you will love us.'

Gillian lifted the puppy out of the big basket. Imogen put down a plate of biscuits and milk. The puppy smelt them and ran to the plate. Soon she was eating greedily.

Then she went to Gillian and tried to jump on to her lap. Gillian let her cuddle there, and she licked her hands.

'Oh, let me have a turn at having Topsy on my knee too,' said Imogen, who loved cuddling toys and animals. So Topsy had a turn at cuddling on Imogen's knee, and she soon began to think that she had come to a very nice new home!

And then Bimbo came running into the nursery to see what all the fuss was about! He stopped when he saw Topsy. What was this – was it Bobs gone a bit small?

Then he smelt a different smell – not Bobs' smell. It must be a new dog, a small one.

Topsy jumped down and sniffed at Bimbo's nose. Bimbo hissed a little, for he wasn't quite certain if this was the kind of dog who might suddenly chase him.

Topsy wagged the tip of her tail very slightly. Bobs had already told Bimbo that a dog's tail was used as a signal for friendship. If a dog wants to be friendly he wags his tail – so Bimbo stopped hissing when he saw that, and sniffed round Topsy's mouth, smelling the biscuit and milk she had eaten.

Topsy wagged her tail in delight. To and fro it went, to and fro, as if it was on a spring.

Then she gave a little yap and ran all round
Bimbo.

'Play with me! I'm sure you are not a
grown-up cat! I'm not a grown-up dog either.
I'm a puppy-dog. Are you a puppy-cat?'

'No, I'm a kitten-cat,' said Bimbo, and he
crouched down behind a chair-leg, ready to
jump out at Topsy. 'Catch me if you can!'

And then began such a chase round the
nursery, in and out of the chairs, round the
piano, over the doll's house and under the
table!

'Oh, look – they *have* made friends quickly!' cried Gillian. 'Aren't they funny!'

Bimbo squeezed inside the toy cupboard and Topsy couldn't imagine where he had gone. Then she smelt the kitten in the cupboard and got inside too. What a scramble round there was! Out flew the small teddy bear – plop! Out flew the clockwork mouse and his key dropped out – ping! Out came half a dozen wooden skittles – clitter-clatter, clitter-clatter!

'Hey! This won't do!' cried Gillian. 'Come out, you scamps! We don't want the whole of the toy cupboard turned out. It's not spring-cleaning time yet!'

The two animals jumped out. Topsy shook herself and sat down, panting, with her tongue hanging out, nice and pink. Bimbo sat down beside her and began to wash himself all over – lick-lick-lick.

'What are you licking yourself for?' asked Topsy. 'Do you taste sweet?'

'Ha, ha, funny joke!' said Bimbo, and went on cleaning himself. 'Topsy, I like you. I'm sure you've been brought here to play with me and have fun. Let's be good friends, shall we?'

'Wuff-wuff, of course we will!' said Topsy, and wagged her tail so hard that it looked like two or three tails wagging at once!

Chapter 3

Topsy Makes a Mistake

The cook didn't like Topsy or Bimbo in her kitchen. 'Now you just go out!' she said to Bimbo. 'I know quite well that as soon as my back is turned you'll be up on the kitchen table after my sausages.'

She shook her rolling-pin at Bimbo and he fled. Topsy looked up at the cook with her soft brown eyes.

'It's no good you looking at me like that,' said the cook. 'You're just as bad. I daresay you won't jump up on the table – but you'll get under my feet all the time, and trip me up. Be off with you!'

Topsy ran out of the kitchen to find Bimbo. 'Isn't it a pity we can't go into the kitchen whenever we want to?' said Topsy. 'It does smell so nice. I like it better than any room in the house, because of its delicious smell.'

'Oh, I know another room that's much nicer,' said Bimbo. 'It's a wonderful room, where meals are always set out ready on shelves – but nobody goes to eat them there; it does seem such a waste.'

'Bones and biscuits, what room's that?' asked Topsy, in the greatest surprise. '*I* don't know it.'

'Well, I'll take you to it,' said Bimbo. 'But you'll find the door is shut. I wish I knew who the meals are waiting for, in that nice little room. I've never seen anyone taken there. If the cook goes there she always shoos me away before she opens the door. But I've seen and smelt all the delicious things through the open door!'

When the cook was out that afternoon Bimbo took Topsy down the stairs and into the kitchen. He showed her a door. 'The room's behind that door,' said Bimbo. 'Topsy, put your nose to the crack, and sniff. Isn't it delicious?'

Topsy put her nose to the door.

'Tails and whiskers!' she said. 'What a

glorious smell! I can smell meat – and fish –
and pie – and sardines left over from breakfast – and bones!'

'Look out! Here comes somebody!' hissed
Bimbo. Topsy ran under the big kitchen
chair and hid there. Bimbo lay down on the
hearthrug. Gillian came into the kitchen and
went to the larder door, under which the two
animals had been so busily sniffing.

She opened it and took out the cake-tin
from the corner. She carried the tin to the
kitchen table and took off the lid. Bimbo got

up slyly and slipped quietly round the side of the open larder door. Topsy saw him and slipped round too.

Gillian was humming a song to herself and didn't hear or see either of them. She took out the cake for tea and put the tin back into its corner of the larder again. Then she ran upstairs with the cake on a plate – but first she shut the larder door!

And she shut in Bimbo and Topsy of course! But they didn't mind. They didn't mind a bit. They were pleased. It was a nice little room to be shut inside. Oh, the smells there!

'What did I tell you?' said Bimbo to Topsy. 'Look at that big meal on the shelf there! Who's it for? Nobody comes to eat here. It's all wasted, it seems to me. Well – it won't be wasted now. Up I go!'

And up on the first shelf Bimbo went. Topsy put her front paws up on the shelf, but she couldn't jump on it as Bimbo did. It was most annoying.

'I'll push you something off,' said Bimbo. 'Just tell me what you'd like. Do you fancy a joint of meat? It's not cooked, so it smells very good indeed. Or there are a few herrings here. And what's this – a rabbit! Oh Topsy, would you like a rabbit? It's cooked.'

'Yes. I'd like a rabbit more than anything,' said Topsy, jumping up and down eagerly. 'Push it over. And push over the meat too. Hurry, for I'm so hungry I can't wait!'

Crash! Over the edge of the shelf went the big brown pot in which the rabbit had been cooked. It tipped over and the gravy ran out. Joints of rabbit fell out and Topsy got her sharp teeth into them at once. Crunch, crunch! Oh, how marvellous!

'What are *you* having?' she called up to Bimbo.

'I've found a jug of yellow custard,' said Bimbo. 'And some sardines. Wait a minute – I'll send over a sardine or two – and I'll tip up the jug to drip a little custard on to the floor.'

Drip-drip – down came some custard on Topsy's head, and two sardines. What a feast the puppy had!

'You know, Bimbo, I really think this meal must have been laid for us,' said Topsy, trying to lick the custard off her left ear with her tongue. 'There are all the things we like.'

Just then they heard Gillian's voice calling loudly. 'Topsy, Topsy, Tops! Topsy, Topsy, Tops! Where are you? Where *can* that dog have gone to? And where's Bimbo? Bim-bim-bim-bimbo!'

'Oh, Gillian is going for a walk!' said Topsy. 'Oh, I *must* go with her, I simply must.'

'Why must you?' asked Bimbo, chewing the head off a herring.

'Well, because there are so many glorious smells all along the lane,' said Topsy, scratching at the door. 'I simply love to smell them every day.'

'Topsy, Topsy, Topsy!' shouted Gillian. Topsy whined loudly, and Bimbo was cross.

'Don't make that noise! We aren't supposed to be here, and if anyone hears us we shall get into dreadful trouble.'

'Why shall we?' said Topsy. 'I'm sure this meal was meant for us! Oh, I do hope Gillian won't go without me.'

But she did – and Topsy was so unhappy about it that she wouldn't eat anything more at all, not even when Bimbo emptied a jug of milk over her and told her to lick it up.

The cook came back after tea. When she

came into the kitchen she stared in amazement at the larder door. From underneath it came a stream of custard, milk and rabbit gravy. How very peculiar!

She opened the door – and out shot a very cross Topsy and a frightened Bimbo. 'Oh, you wicked creatures!' cried the cook, when she saw the mess her larder was in! 'What will your mistress say to you! How did you get in? The door was shut! You couldn't have squeezed under the door or got in through the keyhole. It's a real puzzle!'

When Mistress heard what had happened she was very cross indeed. 'You must both be scolded,' she said. 'Bimbo, you know quite well that cats are not allowed in the larder. Topsy, you mustn't believe all that naughty Bimbo tells you. Come here!'

Scold-scold-scold! Poor Topsy. Poor Bimbo. Topsy crept to her basket and lay down with her ears drooping and her tail between her legs. Bimbo fled away to the nursery and hid at the back of the toy cupboard. He was very angry.

'I'll tell Gillian all about it when she comes in!' he said. So he did – but Gillian put on a very stern face and shook her head. 'You're naughty and mischievous. Larders aren't for puppies or kittens. You know that very well! I am ashamed of you both.'

'We'll never go into the larder again!' whined Topsy.

'Never, never!' mewed Bimbo. So they were forgiven, and before very long Topsy was curled up on Gillian's knee, dreaming of rabbit and custard, and Bimbo was cuddled on Imogen's knee, dreaming of milk and herring.

And Cosy, the tabby-cat, licked up all the rabbit gravy, the milk and the custard from the floor and had a perfectly lovely time.

'She might have said "Thank you" to us!' said Topsy.

But she didn't!

Chapter 4
Bimbo Gets a Shock

Topsy and Bobs, the two dogs, often used to get baths when they were dirty. How they hated that! As soon as Bobs saw the bath being dragged out of the shed, he ran away out of the front gate. So Gillian had to catch him first, and tie him up – and then get the bath out.

Topsy didn't know what the bath was at first. When she heard Gillian pulling it out of the shed – clank-clank-clank – she ran to see whatever could be making the noise.

Bobs was tied up near by. He growled at Topsy. 'It's all because of *you* that we're going to have baths,' he said. 'You rolled in the mud this morning, and Mistress said, "Topsy does smell! She must have a bath – so Bobs may as well have one too, though he's not really dirty." I do feel cross with you, Topsy.'

'Why, what's the matter with a bath?' said Topsy, surprised. 'This thing is a bath, isn't it? Well, what harm can it do us?'

'You wait and see!' said Bobs. So Topsy waited – and when the bath was filled with water, what a surprise she got! Gillian lifted her up and put her, splash, into the big bath. And then Imogen soaped her well.

'Don't wriggle so,' said Imogen, 'or the soap will get into your eyes.'

But Topsy did wriggle, and the soap did

get into her eyes. How she howled! Imogen
poured some water over her head to get the
soap out. Topsy didn't like that either. She
didn't like the hot water, she didn't like the
soap, she didn't like being wet, and she
didn't like being rubbed dry. She didn't like
anything about the bath at all.

'Now you see what I mean when I say that
baths are horrid,' said Bobs, trying to pull
away from the rope that tied him to a railing
near by. 'You've had your turn – now mine is
coming, and I'm not really dirty, either!'

'Will Bimbo have his turn after you?' asked
Topsy, shaking hundreds of drops from her
wet coat.

'Don't do that all over me,' said Bobs, 'I
shall have enough water on me in a minute
without you wetting me too! Of course
Bimbo won't have a bath, silly. Cats never
do.'

'Well, I don't call that fair!' said Topsy
angrily. 'Why should dogs have to have
baths, when cats never do? I'm sure Bimbo
gets just as dirty as I do.'

Bimbo ran up joyfully when he saw the
bath steaming in the garden. 'Ha ha!' he
mewed. 'A bath! I see you've had one, Topsy!

How did you like it? What dirty creatures dogs must be, always having baths. I'll sit and watch Bobs having his.'

'No, you won't,' said Bobs. 'You just go

away. I'm not going to have you sitting there grinning whenever I get soap in my eyes.'

But Bobs had to have his bath with Bimbo sitting there. How that kitten laughed when Bobs yelped that the water was too hot! How he enjoyed it when Bobs whined because he got the soap in his eyes!

'Topsy, how can you stand there and let Bimbo laugh at me like that!' cried Bobs. 'Chase him away.'

So Topsy ran at Bimbo. At first Bimbo just rolled over to play with her, but when he found that Topsy gave him a nip on his tail to make him run, he ran! He wasn't going to have his fine long tail nipped like that.

Bimbo tore down the garden. Topsy chased after him, yapping at his heels. Bimbo leapt over the wall, and disappeared. But Topsy found a hole to squeeze through and soon Bimbo found her after him again.

The kitten tore back to the wall that ran at the bottom of his own garden, and jumped up on it. Topsy jumped to see if she could get Bimbo's tail – and the kitten leapt down on the other side in a great hurry. Off he went up the garden again.

He ran all round the house with Topsy after him, and then jumped up on to the roof of the shed. He lost his balance – and fell.

And, oh dear me, just under the shed was the bath! Gillian had pulled it over there to empty it down the drain. She was just tipping it up – and Bimbo fell right into it.

119

SPLASH! Gillian was so surprised to see Bimbo in the bath. But Bimbo was even more surprised. Ooooh! Water! How horrible, how frightening!

'Bimbo wants a bath!' cried Imogen in delight. 'He's jumped into the water. Let me soap him.'

And before poor Bimbo could do anything about it, there was Imogen soaping him for all she was worth. Bimbo wriggled and mewed, and the soap went into his eyes. Then how he yowled!

'Wuff, wuff, wuff!' laughed Bobs and Topsy. 'This is a great joke! Bimbo laughed at us for having a bath – and now he's having a bath too! Is the water nice and wet, Bimmy? Is the soap slippery? Are you clean?'

Bimbo put out his claws and Imogen let go. She didn't want to be scratched!

Bimbo jumped out of the water. He mewed and shook himself. Showers of drops flew everywhere. Gillian threw a towel over him and began to rub him dry. But Bimbo did not want to be rubbed, and he shot off down the garden with the towel trailing behind.

How the two dogs laughed! 'Did you like

your bath, Bimbo?' they cried. 'Was it lovely? You won't sit and laugh at us next time, will you?'

And Bimbo certainly won't! As soon as he sees that bath being dragged out of the shed, he's off to the bottom of the next-garden-but-one. No more baths for Bimbo!

Chapter 5
Topsy Wants a New Tail

Topsy didn't like her tail very much. She thought it was much too short. She liked Bimbo's long brown tail very much indeed.

'I wish I had a long tail like yours,' she said. 'Bones and biscuits, couldn't I wag it beautifully then!'

'It *is* nice to wave a long tail about,' said Bimbo. 'But I like to wave mine to and fro when I'm cross, Topsy, not when I'm friendly, like you.'

'Yes, I've noticed that,' said Topsy. 'If I had a long tail I wouldn't waste it on cross waggings. I'd have a marvellous time shaking it at every dog I met!'

'Well, I'm sorry I can't lend you my tail,'

said Bimbo. 'It's a pity dogs have such short, ugly tails. Yours isn't much more than a stump!'

Bimbo thought quite a lot about Topsy and her tail. He wished he could get her a nice long one. And then one day he heard Gillian say something that made him feel quite excited.

Gillian was talking to Imogen. She had a book on her knee and she said, 'You know, Imogen, this book has the most lovely tales in it. You ought to read it.'

'What sort of tales?' asked Imogen. 'Long tales or short tales?'

'It's got both,' said Gillian. 'Look, I'll put the book back into the bookshelf, Imogen, and you can get it when you want a nice long tale.'

Well, when Bimbo heard that, his whiskers shook with excitement. So that was where long tails were kept – in books! How marvellous – now he might be able to get one for Topsy to wear.

He ran off to find the puppy. She was sitting by the gardener, watching him dig in the earth.

'Hello!' said Topsy. 'The gardener is aw-

fully busy digging this morning. I think there must be hidden treasure somewhere here, because he's digging and digging. I'm waiting for him to find it.'

'Well, you'll wait for weeks then,' said Bimbo. 'He's only digging a trench for seeds! Listen, Topsy, I've heard something lovely this morning.'

'What?' asked Topsy. 'Are we going to have something special for dinner – or is Gillian going to take me for a long walk?'

'No – something much better than that!'

said Bimbo. 'I know where we can find a long tail for you!'

'Bones and biscuits!' said Topsy in delight. 'That's good news! Where's the tail? Do we have to buy it?'

'Oh no – we can find one in the nursery,' said Bimbo. 'I heard Gillian say so. They are kept inside those things called books. Gillian said there were long tails and short tails there. We'll find the longest one there is and get it for you. Then you'll have a lovely time waving it about!'

'Fine!' said Topsy, jumping up and down and setting her tail going wag-wag-wag. 'Come on – let's go and get it.'

Off they went up the garden and into the house. They rushed up to the nursery. There was no one there. The children had gone to school.

'In that book shelf there must be hundreds of tails,' said Bimbo, looking at all the story books there. 'Hundreds and hundreds.'

'Well, hurry up and find a few for me to try on!' said Topsy, prancing round in excitement. 'Where are they? I can't see any sticking out.'

'Wait a minute, Topsy – what are we going

to do about the tail you're wearing now?' said Bimbo suddenly. 'You can't wear two tails, you know.'

'Can't we find a black tail to match mine, and tie it on?' said Topsy. 'I don't want you to cut mine off. I shouldn't like that at all.'

'All right,' said Bimbo. 'We'll try to find a nice long wavy black tail! Come on! Pull out two or three of these books and hunt for tails inside them.'

So before two minutes had gone by, there was a marvellous mess on the floor! Books of all kinds had been pulled out, and opened. Bimbo and Topsy sniffed and sniffed at the pages – but to their great disappointment, not a single tail could they find!

'Well, that's funny,' said Bimbo, sitting down and beginning to wash himself. 'I know I heard Gillian say there were long and short tails in these books – and especially in *this* book, because she had it on her knee whilst she spoke.'

'I do so want a long tail,' whined Topsy, sniffing round the books. She took hold of a page with her sharp little puppy teeth, and tore it out. But still there wasn't a tail to be found! So she tore out a few more pages just because she was cross!

And then Bobs came trotting into the room. How he stared when he saw the mess on the floor!

'Whatever are you doing?' he said. 'You *will* get into trouble!'

'We're trying to find a long tail for Topsy,' said Bimbo. 'That's all.'

'Well, you won't find one in those books,' said Bobs. 'I should have thought anyone would have known that!'

Bimbo explained what he had heard Gillian say – and then how Bobs laughed! He laughed and he laughed, and Bimbo and Topsy saw all his strong white teeth and pink tongue.

'Whatever are you laughing at?' said Bimbo in surprise. 'Have we said anything funny?'

'Bimbo, the tales in books are meant to be *read* and not worn or wagged!' said Bobs, beginning to laugh all over again. 'They're not furry tails like ours – they are made of words that go on and on over the pages. Oh, what a silly pair you are!'

Just then the children came home from school, and Bobs disappeared.

'I'm not going to be blamed for that mess on the floor,' he said. 'Goodbye – and I expect you'll have a fine tale to tell me when you see me next – but you won't wag it!'

Poor Bimbo and Topsy. They had a sad tale to tell Bobs that evening.

'We got dreadfully scolded,' said Bimbo. 'I feel very unhappy.'

Bobs looked at Topsy. 'I see you've even lost what tail you had!' he said. Topsy looked round to the back of her. Her tail wasn't there! Not a tail, not a wag was to be seen. She was most alarmed.

'Oh, Bimbo, even my little short tail is gone!' she wuffed. 'What can have happened to it? It's usually sticking up straight at the

end of me, ready to wag and wag. But it isn't there!'

Bimbo looked. Sure enough there was no nice little stump of tail there. Topsy looked so funny without it.

'You've dropped it somewhere, I suppose,' said Bimbo. 'Oh, what a pity! Well, we'd better look for it before it gets swept up and put into the dustbin.'

'I don't want my tail put into the dustbin,' wept poor Topsy. 'It was only a short one, but I liked it. It was so waggy. Oh, wherever can it be?'

Bobs laughed. He wouldn't join in the

hunt. He lay with his nose on his paws and watched the puppy and the kitten sniff all round for the lost tail. They hunted under the couch. They looked under every chair. They sniffed down the passageway. They looked under every cushion.

'It's gone,' said Topsy. 'Perhaps Cosy came in and found it and chewed it up. Oh dear, oh dear – Gillian and Imogen won't like me any more without a tail. What an unlucky day this is! We look for a new tail for me and don't find one – and then I go and lose my old tail too!'

Gillian and Imogen came running into the room. 'Come for a walk, Topsy!' they cried. Topsy jumped up in delight. And Bimbo gave a loud meow of surprise.

'Topsy! Your tail is back. Look, look!'

Sure enough there was Topsy's little tail wagging hard. How strange!

'But where was it?' barked Topsy.

Then Bobs laughed and said: 'It was on the back of you all the time, Topsy! But you had been scolded and you were sad – so your tail went right down between your back legs – and you couldn't see it! But as soon as Gillian said "walk" you felt happy and your tail sprang up again to wag! Oh, what a funny dog you are!'

'Hurray! I'm happy again!' cried Topsy. 'I've got my waggy tail – and I shall keep it now and not go hunting all over the place for a new one! Come on, Gillian – I'm ready for a walk!'

And off went the children and Topsy – and you should have seen her tail! Wag-wag-wag, it went, wag-wag-wag! I'm a happy tail on a happy dog. Wag-wag-wag!

Chapter 6
Bimbo Disappears

One day Topsy felt as if she must tease Bobs, Cosy and Bimbo. She even felt that she must tease the white pigeons on the lawn.

So every time the pigeons flew down she ran at them and sent them away into the air again, with a great flapping of wings.

Then she saw Cosy asleep on the wall, with her striped tail hanging down. Topsy jumped up at the tail and nipped it hard. Cosy awoke with a yowl, leapt high into the air and disappeared over the wall into the next garden.

Topsy thought this was great fun. She felt sure that Bobs was asleep somewhere. What about teasing him too? So she hunted around for Bobs, and at last found him. He was lying fast asleep in the shade of a bush, for it was a hot day.

Topsy crept up to Bobs. She came over the grass, and her little feet didn't make any sound at all. She crept nearer – and nearer – and nearer.

Then, with a yelp and a bound, she pounced right on to Bobs, jumping on to his middle!

He awoke, and sprang to his four feet in horror, thinking that a hundred elephants at least must have trodden on him. When he saw it was Topsy, he was very angry. He rushed at her and snapped hard with his teeth. Topsy felt her left ear nipped, and gave a yelp. She put her tail down and ran away.

'I shan't go near Bobs again,' she thought. 'He is too fierce.'

So she went to find Bimbo. She soon found him. He was asleep too, for he had spent the night hunting mice in the garden, and he was very sleepy. So there he was, his nose almost hidden in his paws, lying on the sunny seat at the bottom of the garden.

Bimbo's tail hung down just as Cosy's had done.

Topsy crept up. She blew at the tail, and Bimbo curled it up on the seat beside him. But soon it fell down again. Then Topsy nibbled at it as if it were her rubber bone. Nibble-nibble-nibble! Nibble-nibble-nibble!

Bimbo didn't like it. He half woke up, curled up his tail again and went to sleep. Topsy waited till the tail fell down again and began to nibble once more.

That woke Bimbo right up, and he was angry when he saw Topsy sitting near by looking very innocent indeed, as if she didn't know anything about tails or about nibbling them either!'

'Leave me alone!' said Bimbo. 'I know you were fidgeting with my tail, and I don't like it. Let me sleep in peace.'

But as soon as Bimbo went to sleep again Topsy began to tease him. She tickled his nose. She blew down his fluffy ears. She tried to nibble his tail again. So in the end Bimbo jumped off the seat and ran away to find a better place to sleep in. Topsy ran after him.

'I'll find you again, wherever you go!' she wuffed. 'I'm having such fun this morning, teasing everybody!'

Bimbo ran round the house. Topsy went after him – but Bimbo could run faster, and when Topsy turned the corner, Bimbo was gone.

Topsy ran round a little, sniffing hard. But she couldn't find Bimbo anywhere. Gillian came out in a little while with Imogen. 'Hello, Topsy!' said Imogen. 'What are you sniffing round for? Do you want to come for a walk? I'm going out with my dolls' pram. My dolls have been out here in the pram all morning, and now they want a walk.'

But for once Topsy didn't want to go for a

walk. She wanted to find Bimbo. So she ran off down the garden, and Imogen went off with Gillian, wheeling her dolls' pram.

Topsy hunted for Bimbo again. Soon she heard the cook calling! 'Bim-Bim-Bimbo! Dinner! Dinner! Co-co-cosy! Dinner for you, dinner! Nice fish! Come along. Bim-Bim-Bimbo!'

Cosy appeared and ran to the kitchen door. Bobs wandered up, but the cook shooed him off.

'No,' she said, 'you and Topsy have had your dinners. This is for Cosy and Bimbo. Now where is Bimbo? Cosy will eat all this up if Bimbo doesn't hurry up.'

Topsy looked at the fine-smelling fish on the plate. 'If I find Bimbo and tell him his dinner is ready, maybe he will be pleased with me and give me a bit,' she said to herself.

So she went off again to find Bimbo. She looked simply everywhere, and barked loudly for the kitten to come.

'Bimbo! Fish for dinner! Bimbo!' she wuffed. 'Cosy is eating it all. What a silly kitten you are! Dinner, Bimbo, dinner!'

But Bimbo didn't come. It was most mysterious. After a while even Bobs began to be worried. 'Do you suppose anything has happened to Bimbo?' he said to Topsy. 'He *always* comes when he is called, especially if it's for his dinner. I'm really rather worried.'

So then Bobs began to hunt too, in all the places he knew. But Bimbo was gone. He just wasn't anywhere at all. So Cosy ate up all the dinner, and then licked the plate. There was none left for poor Bimbo.

'We must tell Gillian and Imogen when they come home that dear old Bimbo is gone,' said Bobs sadly. 'Won't they be sad? But maybe they can ring up the police and tell them about Bimbo. Someone may have found him and taken him there.'

'I do wish I hadn't teased Bimbo this morning,' said Topsy. 'I feel very bad about it now.'

'Well, I hope you feel as bad about teasing *me*!' said Bobs. 'You are a perfect nuisance sometimes, Topsy. Oh, look – here are the children coming back from their walk! Let's go and tell them the sad news.'

So up they ran and told the news to Gillian and Imogen. But somehow or other the children did not seem at all worried!

'Aren't you sad and sorry?' said Topsy, in surprise. 'You love Bimbo, don't you? Well, why do you smile when we tell you he has quite disappeared?'

'Well, we are smiling because we happen to know where he is!' said Gillian, with a laugh.

'Where?' cried Bobs and Topsy together.

'Show them, Imogen,' said Gillian. So Imogen lifted up the cover of her dolls' pram – and there, curled up with Angela the doll, lay Bimbo, his tail round him, fast asleep!

'Bones and biscuits!' cried Bobs. 'Whoever would have thought of a hiding-place like that! Did you take him out for a walk, Imogen?'

'Yes,' said Imogen. 'You see, I didn't know he was in the pram – and off I went, pushing it, thinking that Angela was really rather heavy today.'

'And suddenly,' said Gillian, 'quite suddenly we saw something moving a little under the pram rug. Imogen was so surprised. She said, "Oh, Gillian. I believe Angela is kicking her legs about. Isn't it strange?"'

'And then I looked under the pram rug to see, and I saw Bimbo curled up there, fast asleep,' said Imogen, with a laugh. 'I did get such a surprise. So we took him for a long walk with Angela and he didn't wake up at all. He's so sleepy, the darling!'

'And to think we've hunted and hunted all over the place for him!' cried Bobs, quite cross. 'We've run for miles all round and round the garden. And Cosy has eaten all his dinner.'

When Bimbo heard the word 'dinner' he woke up at once. He sat up, and looked down in surprise at Angela the doll. Then he remembered how he had got into the pram to hide from Topsy. He looked over the side at the two dogs.

'Well, you didn't find me!' he said wagging his whiskers a little. 'What's this I hear about dinner?'

'Cosy has eaten all yours,' said Topsy. 'Every bit. And licked the plate too. That's what comes of going off in a dolls' pram, silly!'

'Well, I like that!' said Bimbo, jumping out. 'Who teased me and made me hide in a pram? It's all your fault that I was taken off for a walk and didn't know about my dinner. I'll never speak to you again, Topsy!'

And Bimbo stalked indoors, with his tail held straight up in the air, looking as haughty as could be.

Topsy was very upset. She ran after him.

'Bimbo! Don't be cross! I'm sorry.'

'No, you're not,' said Bimbo. 'I know you! You're a horrid, teasing puppy-dog, and I don't know why I liked you. I shall never like you again. Don't dare to speak to me!'

And no matter what poor Topsy tried to say or do to Bimbo, he wouldn't even look at her. He wouldn't speak to her or play with her.

'What shall I do about it, Bobs?' said Topsy sadly. 'Bimbo is my very best friend. It is dreadful to quarrel like this.'

'Well, you must put it right,' said Bobs. 'You made him lose his dinner – why not give him your supper, when it comes? Maybe he won't feel so angry with you then.'

'That's a good idea,' said Topsy, cheering up a little. So when Mistress put down her supper, she didn't gobble it up, but only just sniffed at it.

'Tails and whiskers – it's such a nice supper,' groaned Topsy. 'Mince and gravy and biscuits all mixed up together. Oh my!'

But Topsy didn't touch it. Instead she ran to where Bimbo was curled up in front of the nursery fire.

'Bimbo!' she said.

'Be quiet and go away,' hissed Bimbo. 'I feel like scratching tonight, so be careful.'

'Bimbo, I've got something for you,' said Topsy.

'Yes – a few more nibbles, I suppose,' said

Bimbo. 'Well, I've got about a hundred scratches in my claws. Just come a bit nearer and you shall feel them.'

'Bimbo – I *have* got a few nibbles for you,' said Topsy. 'But not the kind you mean! My supper is down in the kitchen – you can have it all for yourself. It is mince and gravy and biscuits!'

'Oh, Topsy – do you mean that?' said Bimbo, jumping to his feet at once. 'Where is it? Quick, take me to it – I'm so hungry I could almost eat the plate too.'

'No, don't do that, or the cook will be cross,' said Topsy. 'Come on, before Bobs finds it and gobbles it up.'

So downstairs they went – and before ten minutes had passed that supper was all eaten by Bimbo. He chewed the mince carefully. He crunched up the biscuits. He licked up the gravy.

'How slowly you eat!' said Topsy, with a sigh. 'I could have gobbled that all up in half a minute! Did you enjoy it, Bimbo? Will you be friends now?'

'Yes, of course,' said Bimbo, beginning to wash his whiskers carefully. 'Look, Topsy – I've left the plate for you to lick. There is still a little gravy on it.'

So Topsy licked the plate quite clean, and enjoyed it. Bimbo washed himself all over and then strolled upstairs again. Topsy's basket was there. Bimbo jumped into it and curled himself up there.

'Where am I to sleep?' said Topsy. 'That's not a very friendly thing to do, to take my basket, Bimbo. I thought we were going to be friends again.'

'So we are,' said Bimbo, making room for Topsy beside him. 'We are going to sleep in the same basket! I can't be friendlier than that, can I? When a kitten and puppy curl up together, that shows they are the best of friends.'

'Woof!' said Topsy, in delight, and jumped into the basket beside Bimbo. Soon they were curled up together, fast asleep.

And when Gillian and Imogen came into the nursery, how they smiled. 'Look!' said Imogen, 'what friends they are! I'm sure they never, ever quarrel.'

But she wasn't quite right, was she?

Chapter 7
Bimbo and the Trees

Bimbo didn't like any dogs except Bobs and Topsy. He was used to them, but he couldn't bear it if a visitor brought a dog that he didn't know into the house.

'Strange dogs are horrid,' said Bimbo to Topsy. 'I can't think how you can go and wag your tail at them as you do, and sniff at them, and play with them. Horrid, barking things!'

'Don't you like our barks?' asked Topsy in surprise. 'How funny of you! I think a bark is a fine noise. Wuff-wuff-wuff!'

'Don't do that right in my ear!' said Bimbo crossly. 'That's the only thing I don't like about you, Topsy – your horrid, loud bark!'

'Look – here's a visitor coming into the

146

room – and she's got *two* dogs!' said Topsy, in delight. 'I'll go and make friends with them at once!'

Poor Bimbo! He didn't have any time to rush out of the room, so he had to jump on the top of the piano and hide behind a vase of flowers. He was so afraid of strange dogs that barked.

The two little dogs were on a lead. They were young and wanted to play. They pulled at their leads and tried to dance round Topsy, whose tail was wagging hard.

'Let them off the lead if you like,' said Mistress to the visitor, when she came into the room. 'The cats are not here, so it will be quite all right.'

She didn't see poor frightened Bimbo hiding behind the flowers on the piano. But as soon as those two dogs were off their leads, they smelt Bimbo at once, and rushed joyfully to the piano. One jumped up on the stool and put his paws on the keys – for the piano was open.

'Tinkle, tinkle, crash!' went the notes on the piano. Bimbo was so scared at the noise that he leapt to the top of the old grandfather clock. The dogs saw him and

ran to the foot of the clock, barking madly.

'Wuff-wuff-wuff! Wuff-wuff-wuff! Oh, isn't this a joke! See the cat on the clock! Wuff-wuff-wuff!'

They had loud barks and Bimbo was frightened almost out of his life. He didn't know what to do. He couldn't jump down, for the barking dogs would get him. And the clock was wobbling a bit and might fall. Then what would happen?

Mistress saw Bimbo. She shooed the dogs out of the room and lifted the frightened kitten down. He leapt out of the window as fast as he could go.

Topsy laughed at him. 'Fancy being frightened of little dogs like that!' she wuffed after him.

'I hate their loud barks!' called back Bimbo. 'That's what frightens me more than anything. I hate anything with a bark.'

Bobs trotted up. 'Did I hear you say that you hate anything with a bark?' he said. 'Well, Bimbo, beware! Do not go near the *trees*!'

'Why not?' said Bimbo, in great astonishment.

'Because every tree has a bark!' said Bobs solemnly.

'Oh, Bobs – you're not telling me the truth,' wailed Bimbo, scared.

'Indeed I am,' said Bobs. 'I always tell the truth. You know that. I tell you, each of the trees you see in the garden has a bark. So beware!'

'Will they bark at me if I go too near them or climb up them?' asked Bimbo. 'They never have, so far.'

'Well, try and see,' said Bobs, with a grin. 'You can always run away if they start barking at you, can't you?'

'Bones and biscuits, I was never frightened of trees before!' sighed poor Bimbo. 'Now I shan't dare to go near them!'

And he didn't. Every time he went into the garden he kept to the middle of the lawn, and Cosy was most astonished. 'What's the matter with you, Bimbo?' she asked. 'Why do you always keep to the middle of the grass?'

'I'm afraid of the trees barking at me,' said Bimbo. 'You'd better be careful too, Cosy. If trees bark, they might bite as well!'

'What in the world are you talking about?' said Cosy in surprise. 'No tree can bark – and certainly not bite. Anyway, *I've* never seen a tree with teeth!'

'Well, Bobs said that all trees have a bark,' said Bimbo.

Then Cosy stood still on the grass and laughed till her whiskers shook. 'Come with me and I'll show you how to treat a tree's bark!' she said. 'Why, Bimbo, I sharpen my claws on the bark of trees!'

Bimbo ran with her to a tree, though he was really afraid of it barking at him. Cosy stood up against the tree and scratched down the trunk with her claws to make them sharp. 'I'm scratching the bark!' she said. 'See, I'm scratching the bark. You do it too, Bimbo!'

So Bimbo did – and when he found that

the tree didn't bark or bite, he felt so pleased. 'Bobs is a storyteller,' he said. 'He really is.'

But he wasn't. He told the truth, didn't he? – and Bimbo made such a mistake!

Chapter 8
Fun in the Garden

When the leaves blew down from the trees, Topsy and Bimbo were very surprised.

'What is happening to the leaves?' said Topsy. 'Why are the trees throwing them down? Are they tired of them?'

'Of course not, silly,' said Bobs. 'They do that every year. You should see the garden in a few weeks' time – my word, it will be full of leaves!'

So it was. The trees were almost bare by then, because a hard frost had come one night and loosened thousands of them. Then the wind blew, and down fluttered the leaves one by one.

Topsy jumped up at them. Bimbo chased

them as they flew away in front of him. It was fun.

One morning the kitten and the puppy were delighted to see that there were two big heaps of leaves on the lawn.

'Oooh, look at that!' said Bimbo. 'The leaves have tidied themselves up and put themselves all together on the lawn for us to play with. Topsy, you take that pile, and I'll have this. We'll burrow down into the middle of our piles and wait till Cosy and Bobs come by. Then we'll jump out at them and give them a dreadful fright!'

So Topsy got into one big pile and hid there and Bimbo got into the other. It was nice and rustly down in the leaves. They were soft, and felt warm.

Soon Bobs came trot-trotting by, his tail in the air, looking for Topsy. But she didn't seem to be anywhere. How funny! Bobs was quite sure he had seen her go out into the garden a few minutes before.

He called to Cosy, who was creeping after a bird near the hedge. 'Cosy, come here! Have you seen Topsy or Bimbo!'

'No,' said Cosy, as the bird flew away. 'I was looking for Bimbo. I say, Bobs – I've got such a good idea!'

'What?' said Bobs. 'I don't much like your good ideas – but you can tell me if you like.'

'Well, listen,' said Cosy. 'Let's get inside those piles of leaves and wait till Topsy and Bimbo come by – and then we can jump out at them and give them a terrible fright!'

'That really would be fun!' said Bobs, his tail wagging fast. 'I'll get into this pile, Cosy, and you get into that. Whoooooosh – I'm going to dive in head first!'

And into the pile of leaves went Bobs – and into the other went Cosy! But, of course, Topsy and Bimbo were already hidden there. What a fright they got – and what a fright Bobs and Cosy got when they felt something biting and yapping, scratching and yowling, in the middle of those leaves!

'There's a monster there!' yelped Bobs, and began to fight Topsy.

'There's a tiger here!' cried Cosy, and began to scratch with all her might at Bimbo.

The gardener came by just then, and was most astonished to see hundreds of leaves flying all over the lawn, and to hear yowls and hisses, yaps and mews, coming from the middle of them.

'Those animals!' he said to himself. 'Here I go and sweep up those untidy leaves into two neat piles – and the next time I come by I see them being scattered all over the garden again. I'll teach those mischievous animals to play about like that!'

And he fetched his broom and began to sweep up Bobs, Topsy, Cosy and Bimbo as fast as he could. They simply couldn't imagine what was happening! As soon as they found their legs they were swept right off them again and were sent round and round the lawn at top speed, first one and then another.

'What is it, what is it?' yelped Topsy.

'There's a thing that goes swish-swish-swish behind me all the time!' mewed Bimbo.

The four animals fled as fast as their legs could take them away. They sat under the big lilac bush and licked themselves.

'Was it you in the leaves?' Bobs asked Topsy and Bimbo. 'Oh, what a fright you gave me! And then the gardener gave me a worse fright still! Look – he's sweeping the leaves up again – and I'm sure the wind is getting up. What fun if it blows the leaves all over the lawn! Well – he won't be able to sweep the wind away!'

And sure enough, the wind *did* come – and once more the leaves were flying all over the lawn.

'Serves you right!' barked Topsy to the poor gardener. But she was careful not to go too near him! She didn't want to be swept away again.

Chapter 9
Bimbo Plays a Trick

Once Bimbo was naughty, and Mistress said he must go without his dinner.

'You have sharpened your claws on my best chairs,' said Mistress. 'You have scratched the legs terribly. You know quite well you are not supposed to do that, you naughty kitten-cat!'

Bimbo was sad when he didn't have any dinner. He thought he had better see if he could get some of Cosy's. But Cosy was ready for him and hissed and spat so fiercely that he didn't dare to do anything but lie down a little way off and watch Cosy eat up all her dinner, and then lick the drips off her whiskers.

'Couldn't I clean your whiskers for you?'

159

said Bimbo. But Cosy said no. So Bimbo wandered off to see if Bobs had got any dinner to spare. Bobs was just eating his meal when Bimbo came up.

'Can I have a little, please?' asked Bimbo. 'I haven't had anything to eat all day.'

'Yes, come and have a bite,' said Bobs – but before Bimbo could even lick a spot of gravy, Bobs had cleaned the plate shiny white!

'You are a gobbler!' said Bimbo, in disgust. 'You'll make yourself ill, one of these days.'

'Only if my meat is bad,' said Bobs cheerfully. 'Dogs always gobble. When we were wild dogs and lived in packs together, we had to eat quickly, for if we didn't the next dog gobbled everything! So I can't get out of my gobbling ways, and it's no use expecting me to.'

'Where's Topsy?' asked Bimbo. 'Is she having her dinner yet?'

'It's just been put down outside,' said Bobs. 'Mistress said that Topsy is an untidy eater and must have her meals out-of-doors until she can learn not to make a mess.'

Bimbo hurried off to see if Topsy had eaten all her dinner. She hadn't. She was just running up to it.

'Hello, Bimbo!' said Topsy. 'Look at my lovely dinner! It's a fine big one, isn't it!'

'Topsy, Bobs has just been telling me that once he made himself ill by gobbling up bad meat,' said Bimbo solemnly. 'There's a nasty smell just here. Maybe it's your dinner that has got bad meat in it.'

'It smells good enough to me,' said Topsy cheerfully, and took a sniff at the plate.

'Be careful, Topsy, be careful!' cried Bimbo, pretending to be frightened. 'I can smell such a horrid smell. I really don't want you to be ill. Let me take a bite at your dinner first and see if it's all right.'

'Well, take a bit then,' said Topsy. So Bimbo took a piece of meat and chewed it slowly, putting it from side to side of his mouth as if he were tasting it carefully. He made such a face that Topsy was quite alarmed.

And then Bimbo rolled over and over and groaned terribly. 'Oh, oh, oh! Ooooooh! I've got such a pain! Oh, that meat must be bad. It really must. Quick, fetch Mistress to me, and tell her to make me better. Oooooooh!'

The last 'ooh' was such a dreadful one that Topsy was frightened. She sped off to find Mistress as fast as she could. And as soon as Topsy was gone, that scamp of a kitten jumped up again as lively as could be and began to eat Topsy's dinner!

'That was a good trick!' thought Bimbo, pleased. 'A very good trick indeed! Bones and biscuits, I must hurry and eat this dinner all up or else Topsy will be back and will catch me. Gobble, gobble, gobble! I've never

eaten so fast in my life! Gobble, gobble, gobble!'

And dear me, it *was* gobble, gobble, gobble! You should just have seen Bimbo greedily taking all the meat and biscuits into his mouth and swallowing them without biting them, just as if he were a dog! It didn't take him long to empty the plate!

Topsy found Mistress. She tugged at her skirt. 'Quick! Quick! Come and see to Bimbo! He ate some bad meat out of my dinner and he's terribly ill. Quick! Quick!'

Mistress hurried out of doors with Topsy. But there was no Bimbo there. How strange! Mistress looked all around and so did Topsy.

'Where is he?' wondered Topsy, puzzled. 'And oh, tails and whiskers, where's my *dinner*!'

There wasn't any dinner. The plate was licked clean. It was all gone. Then Topsy knew what had happened and she gave an angry wuff and flew off to find Bimbo.

And do you know what was happening to that naughty kitten? Well, he had eaten up Topsy's dinner so fast that he had *really* made himself ill! He had a dreadful pain in his middle and was groaning away to himself in a corner. He saw Topsy coming and cried out to her: 'I'm ill, I'm ill! Go and fetch Mistress to make me better!'

But Topsy wasn't going to do that again. 'I've fetched Mistress once!' she cried, 'and I found my nice dinner all eaten up. You're not going to play the same trick twice!'

And she ran at Bimbo and nipped the end of his brown tail. She wouldn't let him come indoors by the warm fire all day long, though poor Bimbo really did have a terrible pain in his middle. But it served him right, didn't it!

He won't eat Topsy's dinner again in a hurry!

Chapter 10
The Little Red Jersey

Mistress was making a little red jersey for Imogen. She had done the back and now she was doing the front. Topsy and Bimbo often watched her knitting needles going clickity-click, clickity-click, as she worked.

'Dear, dear! How careless I am!' said Mistress one morning. 'I've dropped at least three stitches!'

Topsy pricked up her ears. Poor Mistress! 'Never mind!' wuffed Topsy. 'I'll find the stitches you've dropped, Mistress! Come on, Bimbo, help me. They must be somewhere under Mistress's chair, because that's where she has been sitting for some time whilst she knitted.'

Well, Topsy hunted all around, with her little black nose to the ground. But she couldn't find those dropped stitches at all! And Bimbo hunted too, till he was quite tired with looking.

'What *are* you two animals rushing round and round my legs for?' said Mistress at last. 'Anyone would think I've dropped some sardines or something, the way you are nosing round under my chair!'

'Mistress, you didn't drop sardines, but you said you'd dropped some stitches!' barked Topsy. 'We are trying to find them for you.'

Then Mistress laughed and laughed. 'You silly little dog!' she said. 'When people drop stitches in their knitting, they don't drop them on the floor. But all the same, it was very sweet of you to try to find them. Don't worry any more, I have picked them up myself.'

'That's funny,' said Bimbo to Topsy. 'I didn't see Mistress pick up anything, did you?'

'What I'm *really* worried about,' said Mistress, 'is that I don't believe I shall have enough wool to finish this little red jersey! That's really a nuisance!'

She rolled up the knitting and put it into a bag. Then she gave Topsy a pat and Bimbo a stroke and went out of the room.

Cosy came running in. Topsy told her about the jersey. 'Mistress says she won't have enough wool to finish that little jersey,' said Topsy. Cosy looked up at the bag where the knitting was. A strand of red wool was sticking out of it.

'I'd like to see that jersey,' said Cosy. 'Let's get down the bag and take the jersey out.'

So the three animals got down the bag and Topsy pulled out the knitting with her teeth. One of the needles fell out on to the floor. And then another and another.

'Oh dear!' said Cosy. 'We shall never find the right place to put them back. Look, Topsy – here's some loose wool. Do you think Mistress knew she had it?'

Topsy tugged at the wool with her teeth. It was really part of the knitting, but the puppy didn't know it. A very long thread unravelled itself. Topsy was delighted.

'Just look!' she said. 'Here's a beautiful long bit of wool for Mistress!'

'Pull it,' said Bimbo, getting excited. 'This is fun! We'll pull the wool right out and then try and roll it up into a ball for Mistress to use. Maybe she will have enough then to finish the jersey.'

So Topsy pulled. The wool came out in a very long string – more and more and more – it was great fun. Soon it stretched right across the nursery!

'I don't somehow feel as if we are doing a very good thing,' said Cosy.

'Oh, don't be silly!' said Bimbo. 'You've no idea how pleased Mistress will be when she sees all the wool we've found for her. Perhaps she didn't know she'd got all this tucked away in the bag.'

More and more wool came out as the jersey unravelled. The animals got excited about it. Cosy tried to roll it up into a ball, but the more she tried, the worse tangle it got into.

Then Bimbo went mad. He often did when he had string or something like that to play with. He raced round and round the room, getting all tangled up in the strands of wool. They got caught round chair legs. They got wound round the table. Soon the room looked most peculiar indeed!

'I don't feel as if Mistress will like this

much,' said Topsy at last. 'I'm sure we've got enough wool to make into a beautiful big ball for Mistress – quite enough to finish the jersey – but it won't seem to roll up tidily. it keeps getting into a terrible tangle!'

Just then the nursery door opened and in came Gillian. How she stared when she saw all the wool wound round the nursery furniture!

'Mummy!' she called. 'Come in quickly! The animals have got your knitting.'

Mistress came running into the room. 'Good gracious!' she cried. 'The mischievous things! Oh, look – they've pulled the little red jersey all undone. I shall have to begin it all over again. Bad Topsy! Bad Bimbo! Naughty Cosy!'

'Mistress, don't be cross – don't you see what a lovely lot of wool we've found for you!' wuffed Topsy. 'You will be able to finish the jersey now.'

'*Finish* it!' cried Mistress. 'Begin it all over again, you mean! Why, the wool you've found for me is the wool I knitted into the jersey! Now you've pulled it all undone. There's a good scolding coming to all of you, if you just wait a minute!'

But nobody waited. Topsy fled downstairs with her tail between her legs, and hid under the lilac bush. Cosy disappeared over the wall into the next garden. Bimbo climbed up to the top of the shed, where he was quite safe.

And poor Mistress had to spend an hour unwinding the wool from the furniture. You can guess that she didn't feel at all pleased!

Chapter 11
Fur Coats in Summer

It was a very hot day. The sun shone down and the flowers drooped in the heat. The birds came to Topsy's bowl of drinking water, and used it for a bath.

Topsy was cross. 'Do you suppose I want to drink your bath-water!' she said to the birds. 'Go away! Go and bathe in the pond next door!'

But the birds came down to the bowl every time that Topsy wasn't looking, and she got very cross indeed. She chased them away every time, and soon she was panting with the heat.

Her tongue hung out, very pink indeed. Bimbo didn't like it.

'Do put your tongue back into your

mouth,' he said. 'It looks so silly hanging out like that. Are you cooling it, or what?'

'I just can't help it,' said Topsy, putting her tongue back into her mouth again. 'As soon as I pant, out comes my tongue.'

'Well, it's rude to put your tongue out at me like that,' said Bimbo. 'There it goes again! Topsy, put it back!'

Topsy flopped down beside Bimbo. 'I'm so hot,' she said. 'So very hot.'

'So am I,' said Bimbo. 'I wish I could get cool. But I can't.'

'You've got a thicker fur coat than I have,' said Topsy, looking at Bimbo's creamy coat. 'Isn't it silly of us to wear fur coats in the summer, Bimbo?'

'Very silly,' said Bimbo. 'Mistress only wears hers in the winter. She wears a thin cotton frock in this hot weather. Her fur coat is put away in the wardrobe.'

'Why can't we take off our fur coats and put them away somewhere too?' said Topsy suddenly. 'Oh, Bimbo – wouldn't it be nice if we just wore our skins? We'd be so cool!'

'Well, I don't see why we should not,' said Bimbo, quite pleased at the idea. 'I shall melt away if I get much hotter. I know I shall. How does Mistress take off her fur coat, Topsy?'

'I think she undoes hooks or buttons,' said Topsy. 'At least, I've seen hooks and buttons on dresses and coats, so I expect there are some on fur coats too.'

'Then that's how we ought to take ours off,' said Bimbo. 'We must look for our hooks or our buttons.'

'Where are they?' said Topsy, screwing herself round to have a good look down the middle of her back. 'I don't seem to remember them.'

'Well, they must be there somewhere,' said Bimbo. 'After all, we've got our fur coats *on*, haven't we? – so they must be buttoned round us somehow. I wonder who put them on us. I don't remember, do you?'

'No, I don't,' said Topsy, looking underneath herself to see if any buttons or hooks were there. 'It's really very funny where my buttons have gone, Bimbo. Have you found yours?'

'No,' said Bimbo, who was licking his fur to see if he could feel any buttons with his tongue. 'They must be hidden deep in our fur, Topsy. I'll hunt for yours, if you like. You'll tie yourself into a knot soon, trying to find them!'

So Bimbo hunted for the buttons that did up Topsy's fur coat – but no matter how he sniffed or licked, he couldn't find a single one! And when Topsy sniffed in Bimbo's coat, she couldn't find any either.

So they went to Bobs. 'Bobs, we want to take off our fur coats, because we're so hot,' said Bimbo.

'Well, take them off then,' said Bobs. 'I'm not stopping you. But go away and leave me alone, because I'm too hot even to talk.'

'Bobs, we can't find our coat buttons,' said Bimbo. 'Please will you look for them and undo them?'

'I can't find my own, so I'm certain I shan't find yours!' said Bobs, closing his eyes. 'Go away.'

The two animals went off sadly. Soon they met Cosy, and she laughed at their long faces. 'Whatever's the matter?' she said.

'We're so hot that we want to take off our coats,' said Topsy. 'But we don't know how to undo them.'

'Hold your breath hard, and maybe your buttons will go pop!' said Cosy. 'Then you can slip your coats off easily!' She laughed and ran off.

Then Bimbo and Topsy held their breaths and swelled themselves up, trying to make their buttons go pop. But they didn't. It was most disappointing.

Mistress came along just then, and was most astonished to see the kitten and the puppy behaving so strangely. 'What *do* you think you're doing?' she said.

'We're trying to take off our fur coats,' said Bimbo. 'We're so hot. Mistress, find our buttons and undo them, please. We want to be just in our skins, then we'll be cool.'

Mistress laughed. 'You silly little things!' she said. 'You can't take off your fur coats. They are growing on you!'

'But, Mistress, you take yours off!' said Topsy. 'Doesn't it grow on you, then?'

'Of course not, Bimbo!' said Mistress. 'We just have our skins and not fur like you. We put our clothes on top, and take them off when we like. It's a better idea than yours!'

'Well, Mistress, it may be a good idea in the summer,' said Topsy, 'but it's a *much* better idea to grow your own fur in the winter. You take my advice and do that. It's lovely and warm!'

But I don't expect Mistress will do anything of the sort, do you?

Chapter 12
Bobs Melts Away

The hot weather went on and on and on. The sun shone down more warmly every day, and the four animals tried their best to find the coolest places to lie in.

Bobs and Topsy hung their tongues out all day long. Bobs grew quite bad-tempered with the heat, and when Topsy and Bimbo wanted him to play with them, he snapped.

'Go away! Fancy talking about playing games when the sun is so hot. You must really be mad! Bones and biscuits, I'm melting away, as it is!'

'Are you really?' said Topsy, her soft brown eyes looking quite alarmed. 'Oh, Bobs, don't do that!'

'Well, I shall, if the sun gets much hotter,'

said Bobs. 'I shall just be a grease-spot on the ground. Then you'll be sorry you ever teased me or played tricks on me.'

Topsy and Bimbo ran off to find a cool place under a bush. 'Do you suppose Bobs really means what he says?' asked Topsy anxiously. 'Do you think he really *might* melt away?'

'Well, he's an old dog and a wise one, so I suppose he knows what he's talking about,' said Bimbo. 'He'd better keep out of the sun, I should think. It wouldn't be at all nice if he melted. I don't suppose he'd come back if he did.'

They lay in the cool for a little while, and then they heard Gillian calling them.

'Dinner, dinner, dinner! Dinner, dinner, dinner! Where are you all! Bobs, Cosy, Topsy, Bimbo! Dinner!'

Cosy jumped down from the wall and ran. Topsy and Bimbo rushed up to Gillian too. But there was no sign of Bobs.

'Do you think he heard?' said Topsy. 'He may be asleep.'

'Let's go and tell him,' said Bimbo. 'It's such a nice dinner. He won't like to miss it, and I'm afraid we shall eat it all if he doesn't come.'

So they ran to where they had last seen Bobs. But he wasn't there. 'He's gone somewhere else,' said Topsy. And then she stopped and stared at something with very round eyes.

'What's the matter?' asked Bimbo.

'Look!' said Topsy, in alarm. 'Look on the ground there, near where Bobs was lying! There's something melting!'

Sure enough, near where Bobs had been,

a round spot of something melting in the sun lay on the ground. The kitten and the puppy stared at it in horror.

'He's done what he said – he's melted!' said Topsy. 'Oh, poor, poor Bobs! He was so hot that he melted!'

'We'd better tell Cosy,' said Bimbo, in a trembling voice. 'Maybe she will be able to do something about it.'

So they ran to Cosy, who was peacefully picking out of one of the dishes the things she liked most.

'Cosy! Come at once!' cried Bimbo. 'Something awful has happened to Bobs. He's melted!'

'Don't be silly,' said Cosy. 'You only say that because you want me to run off somewhere whilst you finish up the dinner. I know you!'

'No, no, really it's true!' cried Bimbo. 'Bobs told us he felt like melting – and now he has. There's nothing left of him but a little round spot melting in the sun. Come and see. It's dreadful.'

Cosy was alarmed. She ran with Topsy and Bimbo and looked at the melting spot.

'Tails and whiskers!' she said. 'Tails and

whiskers! This is serious. Bobs is gone. Poor old Bobs! To think he should have melted away to nothing like that. We'd better be careful ourselves, and not lie about in the sun or we shall melt too.'

Topsy smelt at the spot on the ground. 'What's left of Bobs smells rather nice,' she said. The others smelt it too.

'Yes, it does smell good,' said Cosy, and she put out a tiny red tongue to have a lick.

'It tastes good too,' she said. 'Have a lick.'

And soon all three animals were licking up that melting spot as fast as they could. Then they sat down and looked sadly at one another.

'That's the end of Bobs,' said Topsy. 'We licked him up. I do feel unhappy.'

'So do I,' said Bimbo. 'We shall miss him.'

Just then there came the pitter-patter, pitter-patter of paws round the corner – and bones and biscuits, what a tremendous surprise – there was Bobs, staring in astonishment at the three animals.

'What in the world do you think you are doing?' he barked. 'Aren't you coming to have your dinner? Why are you sitting round in a ring, looking so miserable?'

'Well – we've just licked you up,' said Topsy, feeling muddled. 'You melted. See, that's where you melted.'

Bobs looked at the wet spot. 'You are a lot of sillies!' he wuffed. 'Really, you are. Gillian came along a little while ago carrying an ice-cream, and a piece of it fell just there. I went along with her because she said she'd give me a taste. I suppose you thought the bit of melting ice-cream was *me*! Well – I don't think it was very kind of you to lick me up, then! If I do melt away, I don't want to be licked up, thank you!'

And Bobs walked off in quite a huff. He wouldn't speak to the others for the rest of the day. Then Topsy promised that if ever Bobs did melt, she would never, never lick him up.

'All right,' said Bobs. 'I'll forgive you! Let's go and have a game!'

Chapter 13
A Very Peculiar Thing

Now one day Topsy felt very hungry indeed. She had been for a long walk by herself, and when she came back she ran to the place where the enamel bowls were.

There was no dinner in the first bowl she sniffed at. Bobs had eaten it all. There was nothing in the small bowl either, except a very delicious smell. Cosy and Bimbo had licked up everything there. She went to the third bowl where dry dog biscuits were always kept. There were nearly always some there – but that day there were none.

'Not a crumb!' wuffed Topsy to herself in dismay. 'This is too bad. I'm so terribly hungry – and there isn't even a lick round a plate for me.'

She sat down in a corner, lifted up her head and howled. It was a very sad and mournful howl. It made Bimbo jump. He was asleep in the next room, and at first he couldn't think what the noise was. Then it came again.

'Whoo-hoo-hooooooooooh!   Whoo-hoo-oooooh!'

'My goodness – it's Topsy!' said Bimbo to himself in surprise. 'What is she making that noise for? Does she think she is singing a song?'

He ran out to see. Topsy was in the middle of another long 'Whoo-hooooooh!' her head well up in the air.

'Topsy! Are you singing?' cried Bimbo. 'I don't like your voice. Stop, do stop!'

'Whoo-hoo-hooooooh!' wailed Topsy. 'I'm so hungry!'

'Well, find something to eat then,' said Bimbo crossly. 'Anyone would think you were Tommy Tucker singing for your supper, the noise you are making. You woke me up.'

'You're always sleeping,' said Topsy. 'I believe you would sleep all day and night if I didn't wake you up sometimes. Whoo-hoo-hoooooh!'

'Topsy, don't. That noise makes me shiver,' said Bimbo. 'Now let's see – what is there for you to eat?'

'Do you know anything anywhere that I can gobble up?' said Topsy, stopping her howling and looking at Bimbo. 'I'll share it with you if you can only tell me where to get something to eat. I'm so hungry I could almost eat your tail.'

'Now if you talk like that I won't think of anything,' said Bimbo, putting his tail under him and sitting down on it. 'Now – what do you feel like?'

'I feel like eating a long string of sausages,' said Topsy. 'Or three or four herrings. Or a joint of meat. Or a rabbit. Or a . . .'

'Well, you might know that all those things are impossible,' said Bimbo. 'I believe there's an old kipper head somewhere in the rubbish heap. What about that?'

'No good,' said Topsy gloomily. 'I ate that two days ago.'

'Well, what about that dirty old bone Bobs buried last week?' said Bimbo. 'You didn't want it then, but now that you're so hungry maybe you'd like it.'

'I would,' said Topsy, 'but I dug that up last Saturday and there's nothing left of it now.'

'If only we could find a cake or two in the nursery,' said Bimbo. 'Sometimes the children leave some on a plate. I could jump up on the table and see.'

'The nursery door is shut,' said Topsy. 'I've already been to see. But oh – doesn't a cake sound *nice*! A lovely crumby cake that I could gobble up. Oh, Bimbo – can't you possibly think where I can get a cake?'

Bimbo thought very hard indeed. Then his whiskers wagged a little, and his blue eyes sparkled.

'I know!' he said. 'I heard Gillian say this

morning that she had put a new cake of soap in the bathroom. I saw it too – it was round, like a cake, and it was pink. What about that, Topsy? It must be a cake of some sort, if Gillian called it a cake.'

'That sounds good,' said Topsy, cheering up. 'Let's go and get it.'

So off the two of them ran to the bathroom. There was no one there. Topsy put her front paws up on the basin to see where the cake of soap was. She saw it there, nice and round and pink. It really looked good enough to eat.

'I can't reach it,' she wuffed. 'Bimbo, you jump up and push it off for me.'

So up jumped Bimbo and down came the slab of slippery soap – plonk! It fell to the floor and Topsy picked it up in her mouth.

'It tastes a bit funny,' she said, and dropped it on the floor again. She sniffed at it. 'It smells sort of sweet, like the flowers in the garden,' she said, 'but it *does* taste a bit funny!'

'I expect it's the kind of cake that tastes lovely when it's bitten into,' said Bimbo. 'Give it a chew, Topsy, and see what it's like in the middle.'

So Topsy picked it up in her mouth again and gave it a good chew. But oh, she didn't at all like the taste. It was horrible.

'Bones and biscuits!' she wuffed. 'I can't eat it. I can't possibly eat it. It must be poisonous. Oh, I've got little bits left in my mouth. I must spit them out.'

But you know what soap does when it's wet – it froths up into a lather full of little bubbles, and that's just what happened to it inside Topsy's wet mouth!

Bimbo looked at Topsy in the greatest astonishment. 'Topsy! You are blowing bubbles!' he cried. 'Oh, you do look funny! Bubbles are coming out of your mouth. Look!'

Sure enough big and little bubbles flew out of Topsy's mouth as she breathed. The more she licked round her mouth to stop the bubbles, the more they came, for her mouth was full of soap.

'Fff-fff-fff-fff!' The bubbles kept on and on coming and Topsy was frightened. She ran out of the bathroom and went downstairs into the garden. There she met Bobs.

'Tails and whiskers!' cried Bobs. 'Whatever are you doing? Why are you blowing bubbles! Look – there they go flying away in the air! Have you got a bubble-pipe in your mouth, Topsy?'

'No, oh no!' wuffed poor Topsy, and as she barked, some great big bubbles flew out of her mouth. Some of them went POP on her whiskers and she didn't like that at all. 'I'm not blowing the bubbles – they are blowing themselves!'

Cosy ran up. 'Topsy is blowing bubbles!' she cried. Then up came Gillian and Imogen and they stared at the puppy in surprise.

'Mummy, come quick! Topsy is blowing bubbles out of her mouth!' shouted Imogen. 'She must have got some soap in her mouth.'

So Mistress came – and how she laughed when she saw poor Topsy puffing big and little bubbles out of her mouth every time she breathed.

'Poor little dog!' she said, 'You've been trying to eat soap. Don't you know that mustn't be eaten? Come with me and I'll put you right.'

Topsy put her tail down and went with Mistress. She had her mouth washed out with water till all the soap was gone. How

glad she was not to have to taste the horrible soap any more!

She ran to tell Bimbo. 'I'm all right again,' she wuffed. 'I'm not bubbling any more!'

'Topsy, Mistress has just put down some nice new dog biscuits in the bowl,' said Bimbo. 'Come and have them.'

But oh, wasn't it a pity – Topsy didn't feel hungry any more. 'I feel sick now,' she said, and her tail went down. 'I can't eat biscuits or anything. Bobs will eat them all.'

'Well, I'll hide a few under the rug in your basket,' said Bimbo, and he did. So, as soon as Topsy feels well enough to eat again, she will know where to go!

Chapter 14

When the Chimney Smoked

Once the nursery chimney wanted sweeping, and smoke began to pour out from the fire.

'What's happening!' cried Bobs. 'The fire keeps puffing smoke at me. I must go and tell the others.'

So off he ran as fast as he could, and met Topsy and Bimbo.

'The nursery fire is smoking!' he cried.

'What's it smoking?' asked Topsy in astonishment. 'A cigarette or a pipe?'

'Don't be silly,' said Bobs. 'It's just smoking. Come and see.'

So they all went to see, and the puppy and kitten were most astonished to see such enormous billows of smoke puffing out of the fireplace.

When Mistress saw all the smoke, she was quite upset. 'Look at that tiresome fire!' she said. 'The chimney is smoking. I must get the sweep.'

So she went for the sweep, and he came with his bundle of poles and his big round brush. The animals watched him in surprise.

'Isn't he black?' wuffed Topsy. 'Does he live in chimneys?'

'What's he going to do?' said Bimbo.

Gillian and Imogen came to watch the sweep. He put his brush on to the top of one of his poles, and pushed it up the chimney. Then he fitted on another pole and pushed the brush a bit higher. Then he fitted on a third pole.

'The poles send the brush higher and higher,' said Gillian, 'and it sweeps the chimney as it goes up. See the sweep twist his poles to send the brush round and round – that sweeps the chimney clean, Imogen.'

'If you go out into the garden, you will see my brush come suddenly out of the chimney,' said the sweep to the children. So they ran downstairs and into the garden. They looked up at the chimneys.

But no brush came. The animals all watched too. It was most disappointing. They didn't quite know which chimney was being swept, when they looked at them all on the roof, but they watched every one of them to see if the brush came popping out.

'Sweep! Your brush isn't coming out!' Imogen shouted up to the nursery window. The sweep popped his head out.

'It's got stuck,' he said. 'Maybe a brick has fallen out of the chimney. I'll have to push a bit.'

Bimbo was most interested in everything. 'I think I'll go up on the roof and have a closer view of what is happening,' he said. 'This is rather exciting. Coming, Topsy?'

'Don't be silly,' said Topsy. 'You know I can't climb. My jumping isn't much good, and my claws won't hold on to things as yours will. You go by yourself – but be careful.'

'Bimbo, you poke your nose into things too much,' said Bobs. 'You'd better not go up on the roof when a chimney is being swept. Why, even the chimney itself might fall on top of you.'

'I don't think so,' said Bimbo, and he went up on the roof at once. He first jumped on to the low garage roof, then on to the scullery roof, then ran up beside the kitchen chimney, then on to the big roof where all the other chimneys were.

'I'll look down them all and tell you which one the brush is in!' he called. 'That will be fun. Then you will know which one to watch.'

So the kitten jumped up first to the top of one big chimney and then to the top of another. He looked down them, but he

could see nothing. There was another big chimney just near by so he jumped up on that.

He looked down it – and at that very moment the sweep's brush shot up to the top of it and knocked poor Bimbo high into the air!

'Oh, look – the brush has come right out of that chimney!' shouted Gillian, 'and it has pushed Bimbo off – and, oh dear, he's gone into another chimney! He's fallen into it!'

Sure enough, poor Bimbo had disappeared into the chimney next to the nursery one. Plonk! He fell right into it and that was the last the children and the animals saw of him on the roof. They stood and waited for him to climb out, but he didn't.

'Oh well, I suppose he will come out when he is ready,' said Bobs. 'I expect he thinks we would all laugh at him if he climbed out now – and so we would. He'll come out when he thinks we're all safely indoors again!'

The sweep's brush disappeared down the chimney. A cloud of black soot hung over the roof for a minute or two and then disappeared.

'The fun's over,' said Bobs. 'We'll go indoors.'

So in they all went. Cosy curled up by the sitting-room fire and fell asleep. Bobs went to visit the cook in the kitchen to see if she was in a good temper. Topsy sat down and began to lick herself, for she felt a bit smoky from the nursery fire.

And, dear me, where was poor old Bimbo?

Chapter 15
The Very Strange Cat

Bimbo was in the chimney. He had fallen right into it, and had put out his claws to save himself as he tumbled down and down. He scrabbled against rough bricks, and at last landed on a ledge half-way down the chimney.

There was a pile of soot there, so it was soft to fall on. Bimbo sat there and tried to get back his breath. Soot flew all round him. It got into his eyes. It got on to his whiskers. It fell into his soft fur and made it as black as the next-door cat's coat.

Poor Bimbo! He coughed and spluttered, and felt very sorry for himself indeed. He sat on the ledge for a little while, trying to get used to the darkness around him. The chimney he was in led down to the cook's bed-room, and there was no fire in it at the moment, which was very lucky for Bimbo.

Bimbo looked up. Which was the best way to get out – to go up, or to go down? He really didn't know.

'Well, I came down from the top, so perhaps I'd better try to get back there,' thought the kitten at last. 'I know my way when I get out on to the roof – but goodness knows where this chimney leads to down there. It looks so dark and narrow.'

So he tried to climb upwards. But the chimney was very steep, and as fast as he climbed up, he fell back. Soot flew all around him and made him cough.

He sat on the ledge again and blinked his sooty eyes. He peered downwards. 'Well, I'll *have* to go down!' he thought. 'There's no other way. Here goes!'

And down he went, head-first, scrabble, scrabble, scratch, scratch, scratch! He fell right down to the fireplace in the cook's room.

The cook was there, doing her hair and putting on a clean apron. When she heard the noise in the chimney, she looked round at the fireplace in amazement.

Whatever could be happening?

Bimbo appeared. He was perfectly black from whiskers to tail. He opened his mouth and yowled pitifully, for he was very sorry for himself.

'What is it? It's a nasty little black imp!' cried the cook, and she tore out of her bedroom as fast as she could go. Bimbo ran after her, for he wanted to go down to the warm kitchen.

'It's after me, it's after me!' cried the cook, and she rushed downstairs at top speed. She ran into the kitchen and slammed the door. Bimbo was left outside, feeling very sad.

He wandered up the kitchen passageway and soon came to where Topsy was sitting down finishing the licking she was giving her paws. The puppy looked up and saw what looked like a black cat creeping slowly towards her.

Topsy jumped up at once and barked loudly. 'Wuff! What are *you* doing here! You don't belong here! Go away, strange cat, go away!'

The strange cat came closer. Topsy wuffed madly and sprang at it. The cat turned in fright and flew down the passageway to the garden, with Topsy after it. The cat jumped over the wall, and Topsy trotted back to the nursery, very pleased with herself.

'That will teach strange cats to come creeping into our house,' she thought, and curled herself up in her basket to have a sleep.

Poor Bimbo! He sat in the garden over the wall and felt very miserable. After a while he decided to go back to his own house. He thought it was very, very unkind of Topsy to have chased him like that.

He jumped back over the wall. He crept quietly round the corner of the house and went in at the garden door. Bobs and Cosy were just trotting along together and they saw him at once.

'Who's that?' cried Cosy. 'What a horrible-looking cat! Chase him, Bobs, chase him!'

'Woooooof!' barked Bobs in his loudest voice, and tried to pounce on poor Bimbo. Bimbo gave a loud yowl and fled away. Bobs ran after him and Bimbo went up a tree.

'Woof, woof, woof!' barked Bobs at the foot. 'Horrible, ugly, strange cat! Stay up there in the tree! I'll bite you if you come down!'

'Oh, don't be so unkind!' mewed Bimbo. 'I'm your friend, Bimbo. Stop barking and listen to me.'

But every time that Bimbo tried to explain who he was, Bobs barked all the more loudly, and simply wouldn't listen. In the end Bimbo curled himself up on a branch and tried to make himself comfortable there. But he couldn't.

So he stood up and shook himself – and a

shower of soot fell down, and made Bobs stare in surprise.

'What a peculiar cat!' he said to himself. 'He uses black powder! I'll go and tell Cosy to come and look.'

As soon as Bobs had trotted round the corner, Bimbo shot down the tree – but Bobs heard him land lightly on the ground and turned to chase him.

How Bimbo ran! He shot away like lightning, with Bobs at his heels, trying to snap at his long tail. Bimbo tried to jump up to the top of the greenhouse – but he just couldn't reach the glass roof, and he fell backwards.

SPLASH! He fell right into the rain-barrel at the side of the greenhouse. He disappeared into the water, and Bobs looked up in astonishment. He barked to Topsy and Cosy, who were running up.

'Cosy! Topsy! That horrid ugly black cat has fallen into the rain-barrel! Come and watch him climb out. We can catch him then.'

So the three of them sat around the rain-barrel and waited. Bimbo came up to the top of the water and splashed around a bit, trying to get out. He got to the side and climbed up. He shook himself.

Bobs and the others looked up at him. They looked and they looked!

'Now if this isn't a most extraordinary thing!' wuffed Bobs. 'A black cat falls into the water – and a different one comes out!'

'Magic!' said Cosy.

'It looks to me rather like old Bimbo,' said Topsy, sniffing.

'What! That drowned cat can't be Bimbo!' cried Bobs. 'No, no – Bimbo is somewhere down that chimney still.'

'Mee-ow-ee-yow, ee-yow!' wailed poor Bimbo. 'I *am* Bimbo! I am, I am! I'm not a strange, ugly, black cat – I'm your own Bimbo, very miserable and wet and unhappy.'

'Bones and biscuits! I really do believe it *is* Bimbo!' cried Cosy. 'Bimbo! Where have you been?'

'Down the chimney,' wailed Bimbo. 'And nobody believed it was me when I came out. The cook called me a black imp and ran away when I landed in her bedroom – and you all chased me and called me names. But I'm Bimbo just the same.'

'He must have been black with soot,' said

Bobs, 'and that's why we didn't know him. What a good thing you fell into the water, Bimbo, and got the black soot washed off you, or we might never have known you again! Come along down. We won't chase you any more.'

So poor, shivering Bimbo jumped down – and what a fuss was made of him for the rest of that day. He had all the titbits out of the dinner-dish, and the warmest place by the fire. He *did* enjoy himself!

Chapter 16
The Moon in the Pail

One night the moon was full. It hung in the sky like a great, white globe, and shone marvellously. The four animals were astonished at it.

'I wonder who hung that lamp in the sky

tonight,' said Bobs. 'It's lighting up the whole garden. It's wonderful. I like it.'

'Do you see how it sails in and out of the clouds?' said Cosy. 'I'd like to do that. It would be fun.'

'I wish I had the moon for my own,' said Topsy. 'I would like such a lovely thing to play with. I would roll it down the garden path, and it would give me a light wherever it went. Oh, I do wish I had it.'

'I'll get it for you,' grinned Bimbo. 'What will you give me if I do?'

'I'll give you the big bone that the butcher boy threw to me this morning,' said Topsy, after she had thought for a while. 'That's what I'll give you. I've hidden it away and nobody knows where it is. But I'll give it to you if you really will get me the moon to play with.'

'Right!' said Bimbo, and ran off. He came to where the cook had stood an empty pail outside the kitchen door. He dragged it to the garden tap and filled the pail full of water.

The reflection of the bright moon shone in the pail of water. It looked lovely there, round and bright, just like the moon in the sky.

Bimbo waited until the water was quite still, and the moon shone there, round and beautiful. Then he ran off to find Topsy.

'Topsy!' he mewed. 'I've got the moon for you. Come and see.'

'Oh, where!' cried Topsy in delight, and ran off with Bimbo to the pail.

'Look in my pail of water,' said Bimbo. 'Do you see the moon there? Well, you can have it.'

'Yes – it's really there,' said Topsy, looking at the reflection of the bright moon there. It really did look exactly as if the moon had fallen into the pail! 'Oh, Bimbo, how good and clever you are to get me the moon, as I asked. But why did you put it into a pail of water?'

'Well, it might have got out if it hadn't got water over it,' said Bimbo at once. 'Now, Topsy, remember your promise – where's that big bone you hid away?'

'I'll show you,' said Topsy, and she took Bimbo to where the yew hedge grew. She dug about a little and sniffed. Then she began to scrabble and scrape for all she was worth, and at last, up came the great big juicy bone that the butcher boy had given to

Topsy for herself. It was rather dirty, but Bimbo didn't mind that! He took it in his mouth and ran off.

'You go and play with your moon!' said Bimbo, with a laugh. So off Topsy went to the pail of water. The moon still swam there, round and bright. Topsy sat down and looked into the water. 'Come on out, Moon,' she said. 'I want to play with you. Come out, and I will roll you down the path like a big shining ball, and every little mouse and hedgehog, every beetle and worm, will come out to watch you rolling by!'

But the moon didn't come out. It stayed in the pail and shone there, silvery bright.

'Do come out!' begged Topsy. 'Please do. It must be so horrid and cold there in the water – and so wet, too. That's the horrid thing about water – it's always so wet. If it was dry, it would be much nicer to bathe in.'

The moon shone there, but it didn't come out. Topsy grew angry.

'Do you want me to put my nose into the water and get you out?' she barked. 'You won't like that. I might nip you with my teeth, Moon. Come along out, do!'

But the moon didn't. Topsy sat and looked

at it, with her head on one side. 'Well, I shall put in my nose then,' she said. 'And I shall get hold of you. So look out!'

She put her nose into the water and tried to get hold of the moon. But, of course, the moon wasn't really there, so all that poor Topsy got was a mouthful of water that made her choke and cough. She was very angry.

'Do you know what I am going to do?' she wuffed. 'I am going to tip the pail over – then the water will run out and away, and you will find yourself on the ground for me to play with!'

So Topsy tipped over the pail, and out went the water with a gurgling noise all over the ground. Topsy waited to jump on the moon – but what a peculiar thing, no moon came out of the pail!

'Where's it gone, where's it gone?' howled Topsy, scraping about the ground as if she thought the moon was stuck there. 'She was in the water – and the water's out, but the moon isn't.'

'Whatever is the matter?' said Bobs, wandering up. 'What are you doing dancing round that empty pail, Topsy? Have you suddenly gone mad?'

'No,' said Topsy. 'But a very sad thing has happened, Bobs. Bimbo got the moon and put her into a pail of water for me. I tipped up the pail to get the moon out – but somehow she's slipped away and gone. I can't find her.'

'Well, I know where she's gone,' said Bobs, with a sudden giggle.

'Where?' said Topsy, in surprise.

'Back to the sky. Look!' said Bobs. And when Topsy looked up into the sky, sure enough there was the bright round moon sailing along between the clouds as quickly as ever!

'Well! To think she jumped back there so quickly!' said Topsy, in surprise. 'Bimbo! Bimbo! Give me back my bone! The moon's got out of the pail and has gone back to the sky!'

But Bimbo was nowhere to be found. Neither was the bone! I'm not at all surprised, are you?

Chapter 17
A Surprise for Bimbo

Once Bimbo went creeping into the kitchen to see if there were anything he could eat. Sometimes the cook dropped things on the floor, and if she couldn't stop to pick them up at that moment, there was just a chance that any animal under the table could snap them up!

'Cook dropped a bit of bacon rind yesterday,' thought Bimbo. 'And once she dropped a sausage! Maybe she will drop a haddock today, or something really exciting!'

So he sat patiently under the table and waited and waited. But all that the cook dropped was a fork that stuck into Bimbo's tail, and he didn't like that at all!

He was just going away when the cook

went into the scullery to answer the back door. Bimbo jumped up on to the table at once. Cook was making cakes – but there was nothing there for Bimbo to eat. He didn't want flour. He didn't want sugar. He didn't want currants.

But wait a minute – what was this? There was a little jug of milk on the table – and oh, the cream on the top of that milk!

'Now this is something worth having!' thought Bimbo in delight, and he put his head down to the jug. He put out his pink tongue – but alas, it couldn't reach the cream, because the jug was only half full.

'Well, there's nothing for it but to put my head into the jug and lick the milk like that,' thought Bimbo. He took a quick look into the scullery. Good – the cook was still talking to the butcher-boy. So into the neck of the jug went Bimbo's little head, and he began to lick up the cream greedily.

Then he heard the cook bang the scullery door and he knew she was coming back. What a scolding he would get if she found him stealing the milk. He tried to take his head out of the jug at once – but he couldn't! It was stuck!

He tried and tried. He heard the cook coming back into the kitchen. Poor Bimbo! He jumped down from the table with his head still in the jug. Milk poured all over him!

He ran quickly out of the door, banging himself on the side of it as he went, because, of course, he couldn't see with his head inside the jug!

Down the passageway he ran, and came to the little room where Mistress often worked. He thought he would go in there and work the jug off his head in peace. He slipped inside the room and sat down, panting, the jug still over his head. It was hard to breathe properly with it on, and it felt very tight and uncomfortable.

'The milk has soaked my face,' thought Bimbo. 'It is perfectly horrid. I don't like it at all. I am very unhappy. Now – before anyone comes, I really *must* try to drag this jug off my head. My front paws will help me.'

So Bimbo sat and tried to pull the jug off his head with his paws. But it simply wouldn't come!

'Bones and biscuits, tails and whiskers, whatever in the world am I to do?' thought poor Bimbo, in a fright. 'Have I got to wear this jug all the rest of my life? I do hope not. I'd better go and find Topsy and see if she will pull it off for me.'

So off he went out of the little room to find Topsy. He couldn't see at all where he was going, and he kept bumping into the wall making a tremendous noise.

Bang-bang, bang-crash, he went. Topsy heard the strange noise and pricked up her ears. She ran to see what it was. Bimbo heard the pitter-patter of her paws and called out to Topsy. 'Topsy, help me! Topsy, help me!'

But the jug made his voice sound very odd indeed – just like yours sounds when you roll up a paper and then talk down it. 'Wop-wop-wop-wop!' his voice sounded like. 'Wop-wop-wop-wop!'

Topsy stared and listened in the greatest astonishment. What could this creature be with a jug for a head and a voice that said 'Wop-wop-wop-wop!' all the time? Topsy didn't like it. She put her tail down and fled away to find Bobs and Cosy.

Bimbo clattered after her, the jug bumping against the walls as he ran. Topsy found Bobs and cosy and wuffed to them.

'There's a jug-headed animal in the house that says 'Wop-wop-wop-wop!' in a funny deep voice. I'm frightened! Save me!'

'Don't be silly,' said Bobs, getting up. 'A jug-headed animal with a voice that says 'Wop-wop!' You must be mad!'

But when Bimbo came round the corner with the jug still on his head, crying for help in a voice that still sounded exactly like 'Wop-wop-wop!' – all the three animals were as scared as could be. They fled into the garden at once. And out into the garden after

them went Bimbo, crying for help. It was a strange sight to see.

Goodness knows what would have happened if Bimbo hadn't run straight into the wall. The jug broke in half and fell off – and there was Bimbo's face looking at the others, scared and soaked with milk.

'Bimbo! Is this a new game or something?' cried Bobs. 'Whatever did you put a jug on your head for? You gave us an awful fright.'

'I didn't put it on,' said poor Bimbo, beginning to wash his face clean. 'It wouldn't come off, that's all. And I think you are a lot of mean creatures, running away when I kept calling out for help.'

'Well, we *would* have helped you if only you had said something sensible instead of 'Wop-wop-wop-wop!' said Topsy. 'We couldn't think what that meant, so we ran away.'

'I did *not* say 'Wop-wop-wop-wop!" said Bimbo. 'But maybe the jug over my head made my words sound like that. You go and get a jug over your head and talk down it, and see what it sounds like, one of you.'

But nobody wanted to – and don't you try either, will you!

Chapter 18
Christmas at Last!

'Christmas is coming,' said Bobs to Bimbo and Topsy.

'Who's he?' asked Topsy. 'A visitor?'

'No, silly,' said Bobs. 'Christmas is a day – we all get presents and everyone is happy.'

'Who brings the presents?' asked Bimbo.

'Santa Claus, of course,' said Bobs.

'Any relation of mine?' asked Bimbo, stretching out his twenty claws for everyone to see. 'I'm Bimbo Claws, as you can see. Is Santa Claus an uncle of mine, do you think?'

'Don't be funny,' said Bobs. 'Santa Claus is a kind old gentleman. Gillian and Imogen call up the chimney to tell him what they want in their Christmas stockings. They hang up a stocking each, and Santa Claus fills it on

226

Christmas Eve. We had better hang up stockings too – it would be lovely to find bones and chocolate and biscuits in them, wouldn't it!'

'That seems a very good idea,' said Bimbo, sitting up. 'Did you say this nice old gentleman lives up the chimney?'

'No, I didn't,' said Bobs. 'I said that the children call up the chimney to tell him what they want.'

'Well, if he can hear them, he must be up the chimney then,' said Topsy. 'Bimbo, you're used to chimneys. You climb up them all, one by one, and see which one Santa Claus lives in.'

'No, thank you,' said Bimbo. 'No more chimneys for me. We'll call up, though, and say what we want, shall we?'

'And we'll hang up stockings too,' said Cosy.

'We haven't got any,' said Topsy. 'We don't wear them. Can't we hang up our collars instead?'

'I suppose you think our collars would easily hold things like biscuits and chocolates?' said Bobs. 'I do think you are silly sometimes, Topsy.'

'Well, you be clever and tell us what to do about stockings then,' said Topsy, snapping at Bobs' tail.

'Don't do that,' said Bobs. 'Let me think a minute. Oh – I know!'

'What?' cried Topsy, Bimbo and Cosy.

'Well, you know that the children's stockings are hung up on the line to dry, don't you?' said Bobs. 'Well, what about jumping up and getting some for ourselves? We can easily do that!'

So the next day all four of them went to look at the clothes line. And, sure enough, there were two pairs of long stockings there – one belonging to Imogen and one to Gillian. It wasn't long before Bobs was jumping up to get hold of one.

But he couldn't get high enough. So Topsy tried. She caught hold of a stocking with her teeth. She hung on for all she was worth – and, oh dear, the clothes line broke, and all the clothes fell in a heap on poor Topsy!

How scared she was! She tore off down the garden, with the line wound round her body – and all the clothes galloped after her!

It was the funniest sight to see. Bobs, Cosy and Bimbo sat down and laughed till they

cried. But when Mistress came out and saw how all the clean clothes were dragged in the mud, she wasn't a bit pleased. Topsy got a scolding and sat and sulked all by herself in the corner. 'That was a very bad idea of yours,' she said to Bobs.

But when Christmas Eve came, what a lovely surprise! Gillian and Imogen came into the nursery with four stockings and showed them to the surprised animals.

'You shall hang up your stockings just as we do!' said Imogen. 'Here is one for you, Bobs – and one for you, Topsy – and smaller ones for the cats.'

The four stockings were hung just above the animals' baskets. They did look funny, hanging limp and thin and empty.

'If you go to sleep, and don't peep, perhaps Santa Claus will come down the chimney here in the night and fill these stockings for you,' said Imogen. 'Perhaps you will have a new collar, Bobs – and you a rubber bone, Topsy – and you a ball to roll about, Bimbo – and you a new rug for your basket, Cosy. And maybe you will have biscuits and sardines and bones and other nice things as well! So go to sleep and don't make a sound, in case

you frighten Santa Claus away!'

'Isn't this exciting?' said Topsy, when the children had gone out of the room. 'I'm going to settle down in my basket and go to sleep straight away!'

'So am I,' said Bimbo. 'Oooh – I do hope I shall get a tin of sardines. I wonder if Santa Claus will have any in his sack?'

'I really *would* love a new collar,' said Bobs. 'Mine is so old. Well – goodnight to you all. I'm going to sleep too. And if we hear old

Father Christmas, we mustn't peep! Do you hear, Topsy? No peeping!'

'Well, don't you peep either,' said Topsy. 'And don't think he is a robber or something when he comes, and bark at him, or you'll frighten him away! Goodnight, everyone!'

And very soon all the animals were fast asleep. Bobs and Cosy were curled up together in one big basket, and Bimbo and Topsy were fast asleep in the small one.

They dreamt that their stockings were full of all the things that animals love – bones and biscuits, sardines and kippers, balls and saucers of cream. Ooooooh!

Chapter 19
A Happy Christmas!

In the morning the four animals awoke. Topsy woke first and put her head out of the basket. She sniffed hard. She could smell a lovely smell.

'Oh! It's Christmas morning!' she wuffed in Bimbo's ear. Bimbo woke up with a jump.

'What about our stockings?' he said. 'Did Santa Claus come in the night? I didn't hear him.'

'LOOK!' cried Bobs, waking up too. 'Our stockings are crammed full! I can smell bones.'

'And I can smell sardines!' cried Cosy. All the animals got out of their baskets and sniffed round the exciting stockings.

'A new collar for me!' barked Bobs, drag-

ging one out in delight. 'Just look at it –
brass studs all the way round. My word, I
shall look grand. I wish I had a tie to go with
it, like men wear.'

'A rubber bone for me!' wuffed Topsy, and
she took the bone from her stocking and
tried to chew it. But the more she chewed at
the bone, the less she seemed to eat of it.
Most peculiar!

'That bone will last you for years,' said
Bobs with a grin. 'It's all chew and no taste!
Give me a real bone any day!'

'A fine new ball for me!' mewed Bimbo,
rolling a lovely red ball over the floor. 'Come
and play with me, Topsy. Throw it into the
air and make it bounce.'

'What about my new rug?' said Cosy, drag-
ging a knitted rug into her basket and lying
down on it. 'Now this is what I call a really
fine present. I shall be able to lie on it and
keep myself warm, and you, Bobs, will be
able to hide all kinds of goodies under it, to
keep till you want them.'

'What, hide them under your rug for you
to nibble at when I'm not there!' cried Bobs.
'No, thank you, Cosy. Oh, tails and whiskers,
there are other things in our stockings too –

look! A real big bone for me, full of crunch and nibble!'

'And there's a tin of sardines for me and Bimbo,' said Cosy. 'Oh, I hope Gillian and Imogen come along quickly to open it. I just feel as if I could do with three or four sardines inside me.'

'There are biscuits at the bottom of *my* stocking,' said Topsy, putting her head right down to the bottom of the stocking and nosing about in the toe. 'Biscuits! Big ones and little ones! I'll give you each one if you like.'

She got some into her mouth – but, dear me, when she wanted to take out her head and give the biscuits to the others, she couldn't get rid of the stocking. It stuck fast over her head and Topsy ran about the room in the stocking. The others did laugh!

Then in came Gillian and Imogen. 'Happy Christmas, Bobs, Topsy, Bimbo and Cosy!' they cried. 'Oh, Topsy, whatever are you doing? What are you wearing that stocking on your head for? Did you think it was a hat?'

They pulled the stocking from Topsy's head, and the four animals crowded round the children to thank them for their lovely

presents. Topsy was glad to have her head
out of the stocking. 'I felt like you did when
you wore the jug,' she said to Bimbo.

'Here's a bar of chocolate for you two
girls,' said Bobs, and he pulled one out from
his basket. 'I've sat on it for the last week,
I'm afraid, so it's a bit squashy, but the taste
is still there, because I've tried it each
morning.'

'And here's one of my very Best Biscuits,' said Topsy, fetching one from her basket. 'It's the biggest one I have had in my dinner bowl for weeks. Try it. I've nibbled a pattern all round the edge to make it pretty for you.'

'And I've been into the hen-run and collected you a few feathers,' said Cosy. 'I hope they'll be useful. Good gracious, Bimbo – whatever *have* you got there?'

'My collection of kipper-heads from the rubbish-heaps all round,' said Bimbo proudly. 'They're the best I could find. I hid them in the landing cupboard in a hat box there.'

'Gracious! That was what made that awful smell, I suppose!' said Gillian. 'And, oh dear, Bimbo – Mummy keeps one of her best hats in that box. I can't imagine what she'll say if she goes out smelling of kippers.'

'I should think she'll be very pleased,' said Bimbo. 'Kippers have a gorgeous smell. I'm surprised people don't make scent of them, instead of silly things like honeysuckle and sweet-peas!'

'Well, thank you all very much,' said Gillian. 'You've given us lovely presents. Now let's all go to breakfast, and we'll show you the presents *we* had too!'

So off they all went, Bobs wearing his new collar, and Topsy carrying her rubber bone for another long chew. Cosy had to leave her rug behind, but Bimbo rolled his ball all the way to the dining-room.

The sardines were opened, and Cosy and Bimbo shared them with the dogs.

'Delicious,' they all said, and licked their whiskers clean.

They had a lovely Christmas, and even had a taste of the great big turkey. They had a special supper that evening of biscuits soaked in turkey gravy, and then, full of good things, they all went to their baskets to sleep.

They curled up together, put their noses between their paws, and dreamed lovely dreams of sardines, bones, collars and balls!

And there we will leave them, dreaming happily, a contented little family of four. Happy days to all of them, and especially to dear old Bimbo and Topsy!

A letter from Topsy

Hello, children!

Well, you've read our book from beginning to end now – and I do hope you liked it. Aren't we a mischievous lot of animals? But all the same I am sure you would like to have a game with us if you lived near by.

Come and live next door, won't you? That would be fine. Then we'd all come and see you, and you could tell us what to put into our next book. We'd teach you to play chase-your-tail and bark-at-the-moon and snap-at-legs. You'd love that!

Barks and licks from,

Topsy

Run-About's Holiday

Run-About's
Holiday

Enid Blyton
Illustrations by Brian Lee

BLOOMSBURY
CHILDREN'S
BOOKS

Contents

Chapter 1

The Funny Little Man

It all began on the day when Robin and Betty left their little wooden engine and its trucks out on the lawn.

They had hurried in to their dinner – and had forgotten all about the red engine and its coloured wooden trucks. They didn't go out to play afterwards because it began to rain.

Suddenly Robin remembered the little train and went to the window. 'Betty – we left the wooden train out on the grass!' he said. 'It will get wet and the paint will be spoilt. I'll go and bring it in.'

'I'll come with you,' said Betty. 'Let's put on our macs and sou'westers – it's nice to go out in the rain!'

So out they went, down the garden to the lawn where they had been playing. 'We left the train here,' said Robin, looking all round. 'Where's it gone?'

It wasn't there. 'We *did* leave it here, didn't we?' said Robin, puzzled. Then he suddenly caught sight of a bit of bright red under a bush. 'Oh, there it is,' he said, and went to the bush.

He pushed aside the leaves – and gave a cry of surprise. 'Oh – here it is – and I say – there's somebody in it! Hey, little fellow, who are you?'

The two children gazed down at their engine with its coloured trucks. In the cab of the engine was a small man with a very long beard, pointed ears and bright green eyes. His coat was as green as the leaves around.

The little fellow looked up at them in surprise and then leapt off the engine. He dived under the bush – but Robin dived after him! Betty gave a loud squeal.

'Oh, what is it – who is it – what's he doing here?'

Robin came out of the bush, his face red with excitement. In his hand he held the little green-coated man, who was wriggling

and shouting.

'Put me down! Let me go! I wasn't doing any harm!'

Robin stood him gently on a garden-seat, still holding him. The rain had stopped, and the sun suddenly came out, so that all the garden was a-sparkle with raindrops hanging on the leaves. There seemed to be magic in the air!

'Who are you?' asked Robin. 'And what are you doing with our engine?'

'I didn't know it was yours,' said the little fellow, his eyes shining very green. 'I'm Run-About the brownie, and I live in Brownie-Town.'

'Why, goodness me – isn't that Fairyland?' said Betty, excited.

'Well, it's *part* of Fairyland,' said Run-About. 'The nicest part, we brownies think. Now, do please let me go.'

'Not yet,' said Robin. 'What were you doing with our engine?'

'Well, you see, I'm a messenger – that's why I'm called Run-About,' said the brownie, 'and I was told to take a message to the squirrel who lives in your garden. It's a long way here and I was tired – and when I saw your lovely engine lying here all alone, I thought I could use it to take me back to Brownie-Town.'

'But it doesn't go by itself, silly!' said Betty, laughing.

'I know. But I can make it go all right,' said Run-About. 'I always carry quite a lot of magic with me.'

Betty and Robin felt so excited that they hardly knew what to do next! Why, this little man might have come straight out of their story-books! Were they dreaming? No – two people couldn't have the same dream. It was real.

'Let's take him into our playroom,' said Robin. 'I'd like to ask him a lot of questions!'

'Yes, let's,' said Betty. 'We'll leave the engine here now it's stopped raining, and fetch it afterwards. Come on, Robin – bring little Run-About.'

'You will let me go, won't you?' said Run-About, as they went indoors, Robin carrying the little brownie gently in his hand.

'Yes, we will. But it *is* so exciting to meet someone like you,' said Robin. 'We can't let you go just yet! You come and see all our toys!'

They were soon in the playroom, and then Robin put the small man down on the floor. Door and windows were shut, so he couldn't run away!

Run-About gazed round in surprise. 'Oh, what a lovely place! Oh, look at that little house – why it would just be big enough for me!'

'It's my doll's house,' said Betty. 'You can

open the front door and go inside, if you like!'

But the little man had now caught sight of Robin's clockwork car, and he ran over to it in excitement. 'A little car! Just my size, too!'

He was so pleased and excited about everything in the playroom that Robin couldn't help laughing.

'Oh, what a lovely tea-set!' said Run-About, when he saw Betty's doll's tea-set. 'And oh –

look at this magnificent aeroplane – and here's a boat! What a lovely place this is! Can I come and visit it whenever I like?'

'Yes,' said Robin, pleased. 'But Run-About – can we visit you too? Please say yes!'

'Of course!' said Run-About. 'I'll take you to my home straightaway – if you'll let me drive that wooden engine of yours!'

'Come on, then!' said Robin, in excitement. 'Let's go out into the garden again and find the engine. Quick, Betty, come along. Oh, what an adventure this will be!'

Chapter 2

A Little Bit of Magic

Robin, Betty and Run-About the brownie ran out into the garden. The brownie ran as quickly as a little mouse. They came to the wooden engine and trucks, lying where they had left them.

The rain had quite stopped now, and the sun was hot. 'I'm too warm in my mac and sou'wester,' said Robin. 'Put them in the shed, Betty.'

Betty ran with them to the shed. The small brownie got into the cab of the engine, smiling all over his face.

'How can *we* get in?' asked Robin. 'We're too big.'

'Easy!' called back the brownie. 'I'll make you small! Put your foot into one of the trucks – you too, Betty – and shut your eyes. Quick, now!'

Each of the children put their toe into a truck, and shut their eyes. A big wind suddenly blew – and they gasped, their breath taken away. They opened their eyes.

Goodness me, what had happened in that moment? 'We've gone small!' cried Robin. 'We're small enough to get into a truck! How did you do it, brownie?'

'I felt just as if I was going right down in a lift!' said Betty, sounding out of breath. 'You did some real magic then, didn't you, Run-About?'

'Yes. I told you I always carried some about with me,' said the brownie. He hopped out of the engine and bent down to its wheels. Robin looked out of his truck to see what he was doing.

'I'm rubbing a bit of Get-Along Magic into the wheels,' said Run-About. 'That's all this engine wants to make it go!'

He climbed back into the cab and beamed round at the children. The engine had two trucks, and Robin was in the first one, Betty in the second.

'All ready?' he asked. 'How does it feel to be small like me?'

'Nice,' said Betty. 'But oh dear, the bushes seem *enormous* and those daisies over there look so big that I could sit quite comfortably on their yellow middles! Ooooh – what's that?'

'It's a butterfly,' said Run-About, cheerfully. 'A peacock butterfly, that's all! Looking for honey, I expect.'

'It's as big as an eagle to us!' said Robin, as the pretty thing flew over them. 'Let's go, Run-About. I do want to find out how you get into Fairyland from here!'

'Well, there are entrances in all kinds of places,' said Run-About. 'Sometimes a hollow tree leads to Fairyland, sometimes a rabbit-hole, sometimes a cave in a hillside. But not many people know these. I know most of them, of course.'

The wooden engine suddenly began to creak and groan. 'We're off!' said Run-About, pleased. 'The magic is working in the wheels. Hold tight!'

The wooden wheels of the engine suddenly began to turn and off went the little train, making a rattling noise.

It ran out from under the bush, over the grass, and on to the path that went to the bottom of the garden.

'Oh – there's the gardener!' said Robin. 'Quick, he mustn't see us!'

But it was too late. The engine and trucks rattled past his legs, and he gave a yell of surprise.

'Hey – what's this!'

Robin and Betty laughed and laughed as they rattled past him. They went right down the path to the hedge at the foot of the garden, and through a gap there into the field beyond.

'Hold tight now,' said Run-About, 'we're going down a rabbit-hole, and we'll be in the dark for a bit. Hold tight!'

They held on tightly to the sides of the trucks as the engine shot down a big rabbit-hole. Well, well – to think that one of the entrances to Fairyland was so very near their own garden! Who would have thought it!

It was quite dark in the rabbit-hole, and the children could see nothing at all. Suddenly they stopped at a wide place in the burrow, and saw two gleaming eyes looking at them. Then something soft brushed past them, and they went on once more.

'That was a rabbit,' explained Run-About. 'We waited at a passing-place so that he could get by. I expect you saw his eyes.'

'Yes, I did. I wondered what they were, they looked so enormous!' said Robin. 'Run-About, is everyone in Fairyland as small as you?'

'Pretty well – except for a giant or two,'

said Run-About. 'But you needn't worry about them – we only keep good ones in Fairyland! Ah – here we are – the other end of the tunnel!'

The engine ran out into daylight, and the sun suddenly shone down again on Robin and Betty. They gazed round in delight. Everything seemed the right size now. Trees grew here and there, and fields lay around,

gleaming with flowers that the children didn't know.

Then Robin saw a peculiar tree – it really and truly looked as if it had biscuits growing on it instead of flowers!

'Stop, Run-About,' he said. 'I want to look at that tree. It makes me feel hungry!'

'Oh, that?' said Run-About. 'Yes, it's a biscuit tree. Do hop out and pick a pocketful – they're most delicious!'

Dear me – *what* a lovely land to come to!

Chapter 3

To Brownie-Town

It was very exciting to pick biscuits off a tree. Robin and Betty picked quite a lot and then went back to the train. Robin nibbled one.

'Oh – it's *lovely*!' he said. 'It tastes of honey.'

'Of course,' said Run-About. 'It's a Honey Biscuit Tree. And over there is a Chocolate Biscuit Tree, look. And we'll soon be passing a Sausage Roll Bush – most useful if you happen to be late for dinner. But we mustn't stop any more.'

The engine started off again, rattling along well, keeping to paths or roads, and pulling its two trucks easily.

Run-About was very proud to be driving it.

All the people they met stared in wonder at him, and he felt very important indeed.

The children sat in the trucks and munched the delicious honey biscuits, looking at everything they passed. They went through a most exciting market, where little folk of all kinds bought and sold.

'A fairy with wings, look!' said Betty. 'And more brownies like Run-About. And that must be a wizard. Robin – see his pointed hat and flying cloak!'

Pixies, elves, brownies, imps, gnomes – all the many folk of Fairyland were there. And the buildings were as interesting as the people!

'Look at that tower reaching right up into the clouds!' said Robin. 'And surely that glittering place over there must be a palace?'

'Yes. It belongs to Prince Bong,' said Run-About. 'It has fifty thousand windows, that's why it glitters. And that's the castle belonging to Wizard Hoo-Ha over there. Once it disappeared when a spell he was making went wrong – we were all *so* surprised. But it came back the next day.'

'This must be a very, very exciting place to live in,' said Betty. 'Oh, look at those dear little crooked cottages!'

'Do you like them?' said Run-About. 'Mine is just the same. We'll soon be in Brownie-Town and I'll show you my own dear little cottage.'

They ran into a small town with curious little shops and houses. Run-About stopped at the very end. The children looked at the cottage there.

'Oh – it's *lovely*!' said Betty. 'Such funny chimneys! And a thatched roof. But there's no door, Run-About!'

'No. I have two doors, really, but when I go off on one of my journeys, I make a spell to turn them into part of the wall,' said Run-About. 'Then nobody can get in. I keep losing my keys, you see, but now I don't mind about keys – I just use a spell.'

He jumped out, and took a pencil from his pocket. He drew a rather crooked outline of a door in the front wall, and a knocker on it. He knocked loudly – and hey presto, his pencilled door became a real one – just as crooked as he had drawn it!

The children went inside. What a dear little place! Run-About went to a cupboard and opened it. Inside, on the shelves, were pies and cakes and tarts and biscuits – all kinds of delicious-looking things!

'Choose what you like and we'll sit down and have a talk,' said Run-About. So soon they were sitting in funny little chairs, eating and talking as fast as they could.

'I told you I was a messenger,' said Run-

About, eating a big jam tart. 'When anything
goes wrong in Fairyland, a message is sent to
me, and I have to go off to try and put it
right. I mean – suppose a bridge breaks
down, the message comes to me – and off I
go to find someone to mend the bridge. I'm
always running about all over the place –
that's how I get my name, as I told you.'

267

'Have you been very busy lately?' asked Robin, taking a bun full of cream.

'Very,' said the brownie. 'Too busy. I've been told to take a holiday. If I get too tired I can't do any magic, you see – then I'm not much use in Fairyland.'

'Run-About – come and stay with *us* for a holiday!' cried Betty, suddenly. 'Do, please do! You can live in our playroom, with all our toys. You'd love that. And we'd play with you whenever we can. It would be a fine holiday for you!'

'Well – that's quite an idea!' said Run-About, his green eyes shining. 'I think I will! But I'd have to leave my address with somebody in case I was wanted. Something might happen that only I could put right.'

'Well, leave *our* address,' said Robin. 'Haven't you got anyone who would come with a letter to you, if things went wrong?'

'Yes. Plenty of creatures would help,' said Run-About. 'Mice or birds or even rabbits could be sent with a message. Yes – I'd love to come for a holiday with you!'

And that is how it came about that Run-About went to have a holiday with Robin and Betty, and how they came to share in many strange adventures. I really must tell you all about them.

Now – there they go, back to the playroom in the children's house, rattling along in the wooden train – but this time Robin is in the cab with Run-About, and Betty is in the first truck, waiting for *her* turn to get into the cab. You don't know what exciting things are going to happen, Robin and Betty. What fun you're going to have!

Chapter 4

A Message for Run-About

It was very exciting to have a brownie living in the playroom! Nobody but Robin and Betty knew he was there, of course. He was very happy indeed, and lived in the doll's house most of the time.

'The biggest bed just fits me,' he said. 'And I do love cooking on the little kitchen stove. Do you mind if I clean the house properly? It's rather dirty and dusty, and the curtains could do with a wash.'

'Oh *yes* – please do,' said Betty. 'It's so difficult for me to clean all the little things there with my big hands! You *are* kind, Run-About. I do so love to see you popping in and out of the front door, and waving to us from the windows!'

Run-About played with all the toys, of course, and longed and longed to sail in the boat. So one night Robin smuggled him into the bathroom when he was having his bath, and Run-About bobbed up and down in the boat very happily.

'Make bigger waves!' he said. 'Bigger ones still! That's right – it's just like the real sea!'

He told the children all kinds of curious

tales – stories of witches and wizards, and spells and enchantments. He really was a most interesting visitor to have!'

'I *am* enjoying this holiday!' he said. 'Especially as nobody has been to bother me about anything. Thank goodness nothing seems to have gone wrong in Fairyland lately!'

It was funny he should say that, because that very afternoon a message came for him. It was brought by a robin. He came flying down to the window-sill with a piece of paper in his beak.

'It's for me,' said Run-About. 'Bother! I hope I haven't to go back home.' He took the paper from the robin and read it.

'Oh dear – yes, something must be done about this. The little arched bridge over the stream near Brownie-Town has broken – and it *must* be mended before midnight because Prince Bong is coming back to his castle tomorrow – he's been away visiting his brother Bing.'

'But – how can you possibly mend a bridge before midnight?' said Robin. 'It would take our workmen *weeks* to do!'

'I'll have to think,' said Run-About, and he

went into the doll's house and sat down on the little stool there, thinking hard.

He jumped up at last and came running out of the little front door. 'I've got it! I can easily mend the bridge if you'll lend me your Meccano set – you know, that collection of bits and pieces that you build things with. You made a lovely crane the other day.'

'Oh yes – of course we'll lend it to you,' said Robin. 'On one condition! That we come and see you mend the bridge!'

'Right!' said Run-About, beaming. 'Come on – we'll go in the engine. Take it into the garden, and bring the box of Meccano things. Don't let anyone see us!'

It wasn't long before they were all speeding away in the wooden train again! Robin and Betty were as small as before, and very excited. The Meccano box was in the last truck.

Down the garden, through the gap in the hedge and down the rabbit-hole! Rattle-rattle, rumble-rumble – that wooden train could certainly go fast when it had Get-Along magic in its wheels! It ran out of the rabbit-hole at last and there they all were in Fairyland again. How lovely!

'We'll go to Brownie-Town and find the broken bridge,' said Run-About. 'No – we can't stop at that biscuit tree – sorry. We'll do our work first and play and eat afterwards!'

They came to the little stream and followed the road beside it. But when they came to the bridge that went over it to the

other side, they could get no further – the bridge was quite broken! It had sagged in the middle, and now it was too dangerous for anything to travel over it.

Two brownies were there, very pleased to see Run-About. 'You're our only hope!' they said. 'You and your good ideas! We've only got till midnight to mend the bridge, Run-About.'

'Whatever happened?' said the brownie.

'One of the giants came along and stupidly walked over the bridge,' said a brownie. 'Crash! That was the end of it – and will you believe it, the giant grumbled because his foot had gone into the water and had got wet!'

'Those giants!' said Run-About, crossly. 'Well it's *quite* impossible to mend the bridge, I'm afraid – but I've a much better idea.'

'What?' asked the two brownies.

'These children have lent me a wonderful box of bits and pieces,' said Run-About, and he showed them the box of Meccano. 'It would be easier to build a fine new bridge than to mend the old one.'

'What a fine idea!' said the brownies, and

soon all the things were being emptied out of the big box. They seemed enormous to the children now, because they themselves were so small!

'Now!' said Run-About, rolling up his sleeves. 'To work, everyone! We've *got* to build a bridge as fast as ever we can!'

Chapter 5

A Fine Little Bridge

It was great fun to build a Meccano bridge over the little river. Robin took charge, because he had so often built all kinds of things in the playroom – cranes and bridges, signals, towers and goodness knows what!

The brownies were very sharp, and did exactly what Robin told them. Betty just handed the pieces one to the other, because she wasn't really very good at building and fixing things together.

'It's a good thing the pieces are so light,' she said. 'I hope they'll be strong enough for a bridge!'

'Oh yes!' said Run-About. 'Anyway I can always add a Hold-Up spell if we're not sure. Does this piece fasten here, Robin?'

'Yes, that's right. I say, we *are* getting on,' said Robin, pleased. 'Shall we make half this side, and then go to the other side and make the other half there – and fit the middles together afterwards!'

'Good idea!' said Run-About. So they made half the bridge, one side of the river, and then Run-About borrowed a tiny boat and they all rowed off to the other side.

Betty's job was to row backwards and forwards fetching the pieces they wanted. She worked very hard indeed!

Soon the other half of the bridge was built, and the two halves met in the middle. Robin very carefully joined them together – and the bridge was finished! It really was a fine one.

The children and the brownies looked at it proudly. 'Couldn't be better,' said Run-About, running to and fro over it. 'As strong as you like! It doesn't even need a Hold-Up spell!'

'I wish we could see Prince Bong's carriage coming across tonight!' said Betty.

'Well – we'll see,' said Run-About. He turned to the other two brownies. 'Send a message to Prince Bong that a new bridge has been built for him. I'm going on holiday again!'

Off the three of them went in the little wooden train – and this time they stopped at the Chocolate Biscuit Tree and also at a tree they hadn't seen before, which grew jam tarts just like big open flowers!

'I wish we grew trees like this in our world,' said Betty. 'Why don't we!'

They were all very tired that evening, and the children went to sleep quickly, wondering whether Run-About would wake them to see Prince Bong going over the bridge they had built for him!

But Run-Around was fast asleep too, and it really looked as if nobody would wake up at all!

And then a tapping came at the playroom window – tap-tap-tap – tap! Tap-tap-tap!

Run-About awoke at once, ran out of the doll's house and went to the window.

'Run-About? I've a message for you,' said a small high voice, and a tiny pixie looked in. 'The Princess Goldie was flying home from a dance tonight on her bat, and he stupidly got caught in the topmost branches of a tree – in your world here, too! She sent a message for you to go and help. Whatever can you do?'

'Goodness! *I* don't know!' said Run-About, astonished. 'Wait – I'll go and wake two children here and see if they have any good ideas.'

Then Robin suddenly felt his shoulder tapped and woke up with a jump to hear Run-About's voice by his ear. The little fellow was up on his pillow.

'Robin! A messenger has come to me. The Princess Goldie is in trouble. Listen!'

He told the boy all about it, and Robin got out of bed to wake Betty. Soon the three of them were having a little meeting.

'How can we get to the top of a big tree in the darkness, and rescue the Princess and take her home?' said Run-About. 'This is the biggest puzzle I've ever had!'

'Run-About – I suppose you couldn't make our toy aeroplane fly, could you?' said Betty, suddenly.

'Of course! The very thing!' cried Run-About. 'I've often wanted to fly in that lovely little aeroplane. I've got plenty of Fly-High magic. I'll go and get it. You get the aeroplane!'

Well, it wasn't long before Robin, Betty, the pixie at the window, and Run-About were all in the aeroplane, the children made as small as the others! They were on the window-sill by the open window, ready to take off.

Run-About had rubbed a Fly-High spell on the wings of the plane, and they were beginning to make a curious humming noise. They quivered and shook – and then, with a swoop, the aeroplane was off into the night-sky, flying beautifully.

'Oh, how wonderful!' cried Betty, looking down at the moonlit world beneath her. 'Oh, what a fine feeling it is to fly high like this!'

'Guide us to the tree where the Princess Goldie waits with her bat,' said Run-About to the pixie. 'We'll soon be there!'

How that toy aeroplane flew – really, it was the most exciting thing that had ever happened to the two children!

Chapter 6

A Most Exciting Night

It was quite a long way to the big tree, but at last the aeroplane arrived there. It circled over the very top, and Run-About looked down in the bright moonlight.

A small voice called out. 'Oh, what's this? An aeroplane! Who is in it, please?'

'Me, Your Highness – Run-About the Brownie,' called Run-About. 'I got your message. I'll get the aeroplane to hover like a butterfly just over your branch – and if you stand up, we'll pull you in. Ready?'

The aeroplane hovered just over the bough where the Princess stood, and she stretched out her arms. Run-About and Robin pulled her gently up and into the aeroplane!

She was the prettiest little thing Robin and Betty had ever seen. 'Like one of the pictures in our fairytale books!' whispered Robin to Betty.

'It's very kind of you to fetch me like this,' said the Princess. 'I really didn't know *what* to do! My bat hurt his wing when he flew into the tree – a most extraordinary thing for a bat to do, but I think he must have been very sleepy. I've bound up his wing and it will be better tomorrow. He's crept under a bough and hung himself upside down to sleep.'

'We'll soon take you back to your castle, dear Princess,' said Run-About. Robin gave him a nudge and whispered to him.

'Do we pass anywhere near the Meccano bridge we built?' he said. 'I do so want to see Prince Bong going over it with his carriage!'

'Ah, yes,' said Run-About, remembering. He turned to the princess. 'Your Highness,' he said, 'would you like to see a marvellous new bridge I and some friends built today? I can easily hover over it.'

'Yes, I would!' said the Princess Goldie. 'Somebody told me about it. It sounds grand!'

'Look – what's that down there?' suddenly said Betty, looking over the side of the aeroplane.

'It's Prince Bong's carriage on the road home!' said Run-About. 'Good! We'll follow him and watch him use our bridge!'

So, in great excitement they flew above the galloping horses and the shining carriage in which they saw Prince Bong.

'I can see the river – we're coming to it!'

cried Betty. 'Oh Robin – suppose our bridge wasn't strong enough and broke just when Prince Bong drove over it. Whatever should we do?'

Everyone began to feel rather worried. The carriage was drawn by eight horses, and looked rather solid and heavy. Surely the little light bridge they had made would not hold the carriage and horses when they drove right across. Why, oh why, hadn't Run-About put a Hold-Up spell on the pieces?

The horses galloped towards the bridge. The coachman slowed down a little as he came near.

'It's just a bit narrow,' said Robin, watching. 'Ah – there goes the first pair of horses on the new bridge!'

The first pair was followed by the second, and soon all the horses, and the carriage too, were on the bridge. Everyone in the aeroplane held their breath. What a load was on that little bridge!

But the bridge held! It creaked just a little when the carriage rolled on, but it held! It really was very well made, and Robin couldn't help feeling proud.

'It's one thing to build a *toy* bridge,' he

said to Betty, 'but this one is a *real* bridge, meant to be used. Run-About, are you pleased?'

Run-About's green eyes shone brightly, and he nodded his head.

'Rather!' he said. 'Well, we've been very busy today and tonight, haven't we? Making a bridge, and rescuing Princess Goldie! We'd better get on now, and fly to her castle.'

Off went the aeroplane again, its little propeller whirring madly. Robin leaned back in his seat. Who would have thought that he would ever ride in his own toy aeroplane? It was really too good to be true!

'There's my castle,' said Princess Goldie, pointing over the side of the aeroplane. Everyone looked down to see it.

It rose up high on a hill, quite a small castle, but a beautiful one, with towers soaring high.

'It's got a drawbridge!' said Robin. 'I've always longed to have a drawbridge let down for me!'

'Well, you shall,' said the Princess. 'I want you to come in and have supper with me. I haven't had much to eat at the dance and I'm hungry.'

So, to Robin's great delight, when the aeroplane flew down beside the great moat that circled the castle, the drawbridge was let down for him to walk over.

'You go first,' said the Princess, 'and feel as grand as you like, Robin!'

So Robin walked over the drawbridge, feeling really very important indeed, and the others followed. Then, with a creak and a groan the drawbridge was drawn up again into place. Now no one could go in or out!

What a wonderful supper they had – and dear me, what did Robin and Betty do afterwards but fall fast asleep! Run-About laughed to see them.

'We'll never get them into the aeroplane again tonight!' he said. 'They must sleep here.'

But what would their mother say when she went into their bedroom next morning and found them missing? What a to-do there would be! Wake up, Robin, wake up, Betty, but no, they won't even open their eyes!

Chapter 7

The Little Roundabout Man

When Robin and Betty woke up next day they remembered all that had happened the night before. They had walked over the drawbridge into Princess Goldie's castle, they had had a wonderful supper with her – and then they had fallen asleep!

'We must be in the castle still – how exciting!' said Robin, and he opened his eyes.

But they weren't in the castle! They were in their beds at home. Robin sat up in surprise. 'But we *can't* be at home – we didn't get back into the aeroplane, I know!'

He ran into the playroom to see if the toy aeroplane was back. No, it wasn't. And Run-About wasn't there either! How strange. Then how did he and Betty get back?

He went to talk to Betty and she couldn't understand it either. They had their breakfast and then went back to the playroom, feeling very puzzled.

Suddenly a whirring noise came to their ears – and in at the window flew the little toy aeroplane, shining in the sun! It landed on the floor very neatly and out jumped Run-About, grinning all over his little bearded face.

'Hello!' he said. 'I'm back again. I stayed the night in the castle and flew home after breakfast.'

The children stared at him in surprise. 'Well, then – how did *we* get back here?' asked Betty. 'We didn't come in the aeroplane!'

'No. The Princess Goldie knew a very clever spell,' said Run-About. 'She rubbed a spell on your eyes to make you wake up in your own beds – and you did.'

'But – but I still don't understand how we got here,' said Robin, puzzled.

'Magic never *can* be understood,' said Run-About. 'So don't worry about it. Didn't we have an exciting time last night? I'm getting quite famous in Fairyland now, what with making bridges and flying aeroplanes!'

'Oh – then perhaps *another* message will be sent to you soon, to put something else right,' said Betty, pleased. 'I must say you're an exciting visitor to have, Run-About!'

'I wonder what your next message will be,' said Robin.

He didn't have very long to wonder. When they were out in the garden after tea, playing hide-and-seek, a little red squirrel sat up in a tree, watching. Robin saw him and pointed him out to Betty and Run-About.

'Why – he's come to give me some news, I'm sure!' said Run-About. 'It's Frisky, from Brownie-Town!' He beckoned to the squirrel, who bounded down at once.

The squirrel whispered into Run-About's ear. 'Dear, dear,' said Run-About, looking all round. 'Where is he? Tell him he can come out of his hiding-place, these children are my friends.'

Then, to the children's surprise, from out of a clump of snapdragons came a funny little fellow, his hat in his hand. He bowed low to Run-About.

'Sir,' he said, 'I have heard of your fame, and how you built that wonderful bridge. People say you can do anything! So I have come to ask your help.'

The children gazed at this funny little man, no bigger than Run-About. He was dressed in very gay clothes, and his hat had an enormously long feather in it.

'Who are you?' asked Run-About, looking pleased.'

'I am Mr Heyho, the Roundabout Man, from the great Fair in Pixie Village,' said the little man. 'A dreadful thing has happened, sir.'

'What is it?' asked Run-About.

'A witch complained of the noise that my roundabout music made,' said Mr Heyho, 'and when I told her that I couldn't stop my roundabout just to please her, she was very angry. She flew over it on her broomstick and dropped a spell into the machinery that makes it work . . .'

'And now I suppose it won't go round and round any more!' said Run-About.

'You're right,' said Mr Heyho. 'And I'm losing a lot of money, Mr Run-About, and the owner of the Fair, Mr Stamp-Around, says I'll have to take my roundabout away and he'll get another.'

'Ah – I know old Stamp-Around,' said Run-About. 'A very hot-tempered fellow. Well, what do you expect me to do, Heyho?'

'I don't know, sir,' said Heyho. 'The witch's spell won't wear off for three days, I'm afraid. I thought perhaps you'd go and ask her to remove it.'

'Good gracious! I wouldn't go near a witch

for anything!' said Run-About. 'I'm afraid I can't help you, Heyho.'

'Couldn't you even find me a new round-about for three days?' said Heyho, dolefully.

Run-About shook his head. 'You can't buy roundabouts easily!' he said. 'No – I'm sorry, but this time I can't do anything to help!'

Heyho turned to go, looking very sad. But before he had disappeared, Betty called out to him.

'Wait! Wait a minute! I've thought of someting that might do. Something in the playroom.'

'What do you mean? *We* haven't a round-about,' said Robin.

'Come up to the playroom and I'll show you something I think will do!' said Betty.

And there they all go at top speed. Whatever in the world has Betty thought of?

Chapter 8

What a Peculiar Roundabout!

Soon Robin and Betty were in the play-room with Run-About and little Mr Heyho. Robin was puzzled. What *had* Betty got in her mind? He knew quite well that there was nothing at all like a roundabout among their toys.

Betty went to the cupboard and rummaged at the back. She brought out a great big humming-top! She put it down with its pointed end to the floor, and began to work the handle up and down that spun it.

Soon the great top was spinning all over the playroom floor, humming as loudly as a hundred bees! Heyho stared at it in the greatest delight.

'Why – that's a perfect roundabout – with its own lovely humming music too!'

'Yes. That's what I thought,' said Betty, pleased. 'Do you think you could use it for a roundabout at your Fair till the witch's spell has worn off your own?'

'Yes – certainly I could!' said Heyho. 'But how could I spin it to make it go round? I'm not big or strong enough.'

'I'll put a Spin Spell into it,' said Run-About. 'Then it will spin itself whenever you say "Spin, top, spin!"'

'Oh – thank you very much,' said Heyho, delighted. 'Can we take it now? How can we get it to the Fair?'

'We could take it in the wooden engine,' said Robin. 'In the second truck. Come on – let's all go. I'll have a ride on the Humming-Top Roundabout too!'

'I say! What fun!' said Betty, thrilled. 'Can we do anything else, Mr Heyho?'

'You can do anything you like,' said Heyho, so happy that he was full of smiles. 'You can go on the swings and down the slippery-slip and throw hoopla rings to see if you can get a prize, and have a go at the coconut shy, and . . .'

'Oh quick, I can't wait! Do come along!' cried Betty. 'Where's the engine? Engine, we're off to Fairyland again!'

And soon away they went as usual, carrying the big top in the second truck. Betty stood in the first truck, as soon as she had been made small enough, and held the top steady, because it rolled round and round in the truck, and she was afraid it might be bumped out, and lost down the rabbit-hole.

It didn't take them very long to arrive at the Fair. It really was a fine one! There was a row of swings that went to and fro and up and down. There was a long and winding slippery-slip packed with squealing pixies. There was a coconut shy where many brownies were throwing balls at rows of coconuts standing on pegs.

And there was the roundabout, of course, but it stood still and silent. No music came from it, and no movement. All round it stood the little folk, looking very sad because they couldn't have a ride on the lovely roundabout.

A man came stamping up, looking very cross. It was the owner of the Fair, Mr Stamp-Around.

'Hey, there!' he called. 'You've got to remove that roundabout. I want to put something else there. It's no use at all, that roundabout of yours, Heyho.'

'I've found the very newest kind of roundabout there is!' shouted back Heyho. 'It makes its own music – and sounds like a hundred bees!'

He and Run-About stood the great humming-top on its foot. Run-About rubbed a powerful spell all round it.

> *'Now begin*
> *To spin, top, spin,*
> *Go round and round,*
> *With humming sound,*
> *And tumble people on the ground!'*

The children heard him whispering this rhyme as he rubbed his magic on to the top. A low humming sound began to come from it.

'Climb up and hold on! The new round-about is about to spin!' cried Heyho. 'A penny a spin! Only a penny!'

Soon the top was crowded with dozens of little folk, all laughing and chattering. What a peculiar roundabout!

'Spin, top, spin!' said Heyho – and at once the great top began to spin round and round, slowly at first, and then faster and faster! It hummed louder still, and an old woman nearby looked round and about, expecting to see a swarm of bees. But it was only the top humming!

What fun it was! And when the top slowed down, sending all the little folk rolling on the ground, how they laughed and shouted.

'It's a grand roundabout!' they said. 'Let's go on it again!'

But this time Betty, Robin and Run-About were the only ones allowed on. How Betty squealed when the top went faster and faster, and filled her ears with its humming!

They all enjoyed it very much, and tumbled off happily when the top slowed down and rolled over. 'Now let's try the other things!' said Robin.

And off they went to swing on the swings, and slide down the winding slippery-slip, and throw the wooden balls at the coconuts. Robin won a big one, and so did Run-About. Betty threw a hoop at the hoopla stall, and it fell exactly round a lovely little brooch. The hoopla man pinned it on her dress. She was so pleased.

They didn't want to leave the exciting Fair but they dared not be late for their dinner. What would they say if Mummy asked them where they had been that morning? She would never believe them if they told her that they had taken their humming-top to a Fair and made it into a roundabout!

'You are a most exciting friend to have, Run-About,' said Robin, as they went back in the little wooden train. 'I do wonder what will happen next?'

Chapter 9

Tiptoe Tells Her Tale

For two days nothing happened at all, and the children were quite disappointed. Then somebody came to see Run-About, someone who looked most upset.

It was a pretty little pixie looking rather like the fairy doll who always stood at the top of the children's tree each Christmas. Run-About knew her at once, when she flew down into the playroom, where he was watching the children build with bricks.

He jumped up quickly. 'Oh – Tiptoe! What's the matter? You're crying!'

The children looked at the pretty little thing and wished their hankies were small enough to wipe her eyes. She rubbed away her tears and tried to smile.

'Oh, Run-About – I'm sorry, to burst in like this, but it's very, very urgent.'

'Tell me,' said Run-About. 'Nothing has happened to your sisters, has it?'

'Yes. Something dreadful!' said Tiptoe. 'I was out shopping today when the Enchanter Frown-Hard came along to our cottage and saw my sisters playing in the garden. And he's captured them all and taken them away!'

'How shocking!' said Run-About, in dismay. 'They'll be so frightened. Where has he taken them?'

'To the tower that reaches the clouds,' said Tiptoe. 'You know the one, don't you – its tip goes right up to the highest clouds. And he's going to keep them prisoners there just because the ball they were playing with hit him on his horrid long nose!'

'We must rescue them,' said Run-About at once.

'But how, dear Run-About?' said Tiptoe. 'We can't get into the tower, because he has taken the door away by magic – it's just brick wall all round.'

'I'll put another one there,' said Tiptoe, valiantly.

'But listen – after Frown-Hard had sent them all up to the very top of the tower, he made the *stairs* disappear too,' said Tiptoe, beginning to cry again. 'So it's just no good trying to get into the tower.'

'The aeroplane!' suddenly said Betty. 'Couldn't we fly to the top of the tower in that and rescue them?'

'No. The Enchanter thought of that,' said Tiptoe, sadly. 'He's got someone watching out for aeroplanes. He's already caught one, with my uncle in it. Oh dear – what are we to do?'

'Perhaps he wouldn't see an aeroplane at night?' said Betty. 'Could we go then, do you think?'

'No. He'd hear it,' said Tiptoe. Then she suddenly smiled. 'Oh! *I* know! I know something that would fly to the top of the tower without a sound!'

'Who? What?' cried Run-About, excited.

'A kite!' said Tiptoe. 'A kite on a very long string. Have these children got a kite? Oh, do say yes!'

They had, of course, and they at once went to their toy cupboard to find it. They pulled it out – a big flat kite with a smiling face and a long tail made of newspaper screwed up into pieces.

'Here it is,' said Betty, pleased. 'But Run-About, you mustn't make this kite small when you get to Fairyland, or it would never take all Tiptoe's sisters! And how are they to come down on it? They would tumble off.'

'Easy,' said Run-About, 'the kite must fly higher than the tower, and flap its long tail against the top window. Then each little sister can climb out and hang on to a bit of the tail! Then off the kite flies to our land!'

'Oh *yes*!' said Tiptoe. 'Let's send a bee to hum the news to my sisters. The Enchanter would never notice such a small creature at the top of the tower!'

'We must wait till the evening,' said Run-About. 'It's no good flying a kite in the day-time – it would certainly be seen.'

It was hard to wait so long, and Tiptoe sighed all day, thinking of her small scared sisters. They sent a message by a big bumble-bee and he came back to say that he had told the little pixies the news, and they would be sure to look out for the kite that night.

Once more the children and Run-About set off in the wooden engine. It was difficult to take the big kite down the rabbit-hole, so Run-About went a different way. He took them through a cave in a distant hill – and hey presto, when they came out of the big tunnel in the hill, they found themselves not far from the Meccano bridge that they had built over the river.

'It's still there!' said Robin, in delight. 'Let's drive over it in the engine.'

So they trundled over the bridge they had built, and it didn't even shake! Then on they went till they came to the Enchanter's castle, gleaming in the moonlight.

Some distance away was the high tower, soaring right up to the clouds. Goodness, how tall it was! But the kite wouldn't mind that – it liked flying high!

Run-About had a very big ball of string. He would need a lot if the kite was to fly as high as the clouds!

The wind blew a little and the kite tried to get out of the truck. 'All right – be patient – you're soon going to fly!' said Run-About. 'We'd better be very, very quiet now, every-one!'

The kite was taken from the truck. It seemed very big to the children now, because, as usual, they had gone small as soon as they got into the train. It took all four of them to pull the kite into position so that the wind could take it.

'We'd better all of us hang on to the string,' said Run-About. 'My word – there it goes up into the air. Fly to the topmost win-dow of the tower, kite – that's right – higher and higher – you're nearly there!'

Chapter 10

What an Exciting Time!

The kite rose high in the wind, and tugged so hard at the string that the children and Run-About were almost jerked off their feet. Little Tiptoe was pulled a few feet into the air, but Betty just dragged her down in time!

The string ran quickly through their fingers as the kite rose higher and higher, and nobody dared to hold it back now. Was the kite at the topmost window yet?

Yes, it was! It had reached the clouds, and its long paper tail tapped against the topmost tower window. Someone opened it cautiously.

Then, one by one, seven tiny little people climbed out, holding on to the tail of the kite. The first one sat down on the first bit of paper, the next one sat down on the second, and so on.

'Hold tight to the string of the tail,' whispered the first little sister. 'Hold tight!'

Down below Tiptoe was waiting anxiously. She was too far away to see her sisters creeping out of the tower window – but the four down below felt each little bump as the seven sisters sat themselves on the bits of paper that made the kite's tail.

'One – two – three – four – five – six – seven – they're all out of the window now, safely on the kite's tail!' said Tiptoe. 'Pull the kite down! Then we'll have them down here with us in no time, and can escape in the wooden train!'

But oh dear, oh dear, who should come up behind them just at that very moment but the horrid old Enchanter!

'Aha!' he said. 'I've been watching your clever little trick. But it won't do, you know. I'll help you to pull down the kite – and I'll capture those seven little sisters again as soon as the kite reaches the ground. And I'll have Tiptoe as well this time!'

What a dreadful shock for everyone! But Run-About was not going to have the little pixie sisters caught again. He whipped out his knife and cut the string of the kite. At once it soared high into the air, and flew off all by itself into the sky – and it took the seven little sisters with it, hanging on its tail!

'Quick, quick! Into the train!' cried Run-About, and they all leapt in. The Enchanter was so surprised by the disappearance of the kite that he didn't even try to stop them!

Off they went through the night at top speed and didn't stop till they came into the garden again. Tiptoe was crying.

'I know my sisters have escaped from the Enchanter – but I'm sure I shall never see them again!' she sobbed.

'Don't be silly,' said Run-About. 'I rubbed a Come-Back spell on the kite before I sent it up into the air. You surely might have guessed that, Tiptoe.'

'Well, I didn't,' said Tiptoe. 'Oh, how clever you are, Run-About. When will the kite come back?'

'I've no idea,' said Run-About. 'All I know is that it *will* come back, and will bring your sisters with it.'

He took Tiptoe into the playroom with him, and she got into one of the dolls' cots with a doll, though she was sure she wouldn't go to sleep! Run-About went to the doll's house and cuddled down into bed, quite tired out.

The children went to bed too, and when Betty heard a leaf tap-tapping against her window, she quite thought it was the kite, and got up to see.

But it wasn't! It hadn't come back the next morning either, and Run-About felt quite worried. Tiptoe cried and cried, and Betty gave her two tiny hankies belonging to her dolls.

They had to go out for a walk that morning, though they didn't want to leave Run-About and Tiptoe. But Mummy said it was lovely and fine, and the wind was very fresh, and they really must go out!

And will you believe it, just as they crossed the field that led to the farm, they saw a kite tangled in a tree! Was it theirs? Could it be?

Yes – it was! How wonderful! Where were the tiny sisters? Were they hurt?

They ran to the tree and climbed up. Yes, it *was* their kite, its string wrapped round and round some twigs. It really was a business to untie it! But where in the world were Tiptoe's sisters?

Betty suddenly saw them! They were all cuddled up in an old blackbird's nest, fast asleep! How sweet they looked!

'There they are – tired out!' said Betty. 'Robin, can you take the nest gently out of its place? We could carry all the little things quite safely home in the nest!'

Robin removed the old nest gently, and carried home the sleeping pixies. Betty took the kite. 'The Come-Back spell can't have been quite strong enough!' she said. 'You *nearly* got home, kite, but not quite!'

How pleased Run-About and Tiptoe were to see the seven little sisters asleep in the nest! Run-About couldn't help laughing out loud – and that woke them up!

The children loved them. They were as frisky and lively as kittens, and did the maddest things. Tiptoe decided that for one night they would all stay in the doll's house before they went back home.

And you should have seen those tiny creatures running in and out of the front door, opening and shutting the windows, cooking on the little stove, and sitting on the little chairs!

But best of all was when Betty looked through the windows at night and saw them all cuddled up into the little beds, fast asleep. I wish *we* could have seen them too, don't you?

Chapter 11

Where is Run-About?

The children felt quite sad when Tiptoe and her seven tiny sisters went home together. Run-About took them in the little wooden train, and Robin and Betty wished they could go with them, but their Granny was coming to see them that day, so they couldn't.

'You'll come back, won't you, Run-About?' said Betty, anxiously, when he got into the cab of the engine. He nodded gaily.

'Oh yes – I haven't finished my holiday with you yet! I feel much better already. I love your doll's house, it's just right for me!'

Off they went, and the children watched them go through the gap in the hedge. 'They'll be going down the rabbit-hole now,' said Betty. 'My word – wouldn't other children love to know that there are secret ways into Fairyland all over the place – if you know where to look for them!'

'We know two already,' said Robin. 'The one down the rabbit-hole and the one through the cave in the hill.'

'Of course, some of the entrances to Fairyland are too small for us to use, unless we're lucky enough to know someone like Run-About, who knows a Go-Small spell,' said Betty. 'Look – there's Granny already!'

They ran to meet their Granny, and had a lovely day with her – but all the time they were listening for Run-About to come back. They had become very fond of the green-eyed brownie, with his long, silky beard and happy ways.

He didn't come back to dinner and he didn't come back to tea, because they looked in the doll's house to see. The wooden engine wasn't back either.

'I expect he's spending the day with Tiptoe and her sisters,' said Robin. 'They really are very sweet!'

Even when bedtime came near Run-About wasn't back. The children felt sad. 'We can't possibly go and see him,' said Robin, mournfully. 'We don't know the Go-Small spell, and if we tried to find the way through that cave in the hill by ourselves, we might lose ourselves.'

'Listen – there's an owl hooting outside,' said Betty, suddenly. 'He sounds as if he's very close. Could he be bringing a message for us, do you think?'

Robin went to the window. A large owl sat on a branch outside, his big eyes gleaming as

he waited. In his sharp curved beak was a scrap of paper. He dropped it when he saw the children, spread his soft wings and flew off silently.

'Yes – it *is* a message!' said Robin, excited. 'Oh goodness me – Granny has spotted it too. She's picking it up and reading it!'

He ran down the stairs, and Granny came in from the garden at the same time, holding the scrap of paper. She held it out to Robin.

'I was just walking round the garden in the evening sunshine, when this note dropped at my feet,' she said, sounding puzzled. 'Is it for you? It must be from one of your friends, though where it came from I really don't know. Perhaps the wind brought it!'

Robin took the note and read it. 'Yes, Granny,' he said, 'it *is* from one of our friends. Thank you. I'll just go and tell Betty.'

Off he went, and he and Betty read the note together. It was from Run-About.

Shall not be home tonight, as Tiptoe is giving a tea-party at midnight to her aunt, Lady High-and-Mighty, who is passing through her village. She is half a witch, and rides on a very fine broomstick with a handle made of gold, and bristles of pure silk! I wish you could come to the party too, but Tiptoe only has ten cups and saucers – that will be seven for her sisters, and one each for herself and for me and for her aunt! She sends her love. See you tomorrow.

Your friend, Run-About.

'Oh! I do *wish* we could go to the party too!' said Betty. 'A midnight party in Fairyland, with Tiptoe and her sisters – and a guest who is half a witch.'

'She'll come riding down on her golden broomstick!' said Robin. 'Listen – there's Mummy calling. We'd better get ready for bed at once!'

They were soon asleep – but, at just about half-past eleven there came a rattling up the garden path. Robin heard it in his sleep, and awoke suddenly. He knew that rattling noise! It was the sound made by the wheels of the little wooden train. Run-About must be back!

He sat up in bed, and soon heard the patter of tiny feet in his bedroom. 'Robin! Are you awake?' said Run-About's voice. 'I want your help. Something dreadful has happened!'

'What?' asked Robin.

'Well, you know that Tiptoe was giving a midnight party for her aunt, don't you? She had just set the table with all the cups and saucers and plates, when suddenly one leg of the table collapsed – and everything fell to the floor and was smashed!'

'Oh dear – what a pity!' said Robin.

'Yes – because there are no shops open to buy another tea-set,' said Run-About. 'So I wondered if Betty would lend us her lovely doll's tea-set, Robin – it's got twelve cups and saucers and plates, hasn't it?'

'Oh yes! Betty would love to lend it to Tiptoe for her party!' said Robin. 'Let's go and tell her.'

'And, as there are *twelve* cups and saucers, would you and Betty like to come to the party too?' said Run-About as they went into Betty's room. 'Tiptoe only had ten, so she couldn't ask you – but if we have twelve, you could come too. Please do!'

'We'll come! We'll *love* to come!' said Robin in excitement. 'Oh, *what* an adventure!'

Chapter 12

A Midnight Party

Betty was just as excited as Robin was, when she was awakened and told the news. She scrambled out of bed at once.

'I'll get the tea-set now. What a good thing nothing is broken – there are twelve of everything still, and a lovely teapot and milk-jug and sugar-basin. Oh, I *never* thought we could use it properly, like this! What fun to be as small as you, Run-About, and drink from my own tiny tea-set!'

'Come in your dressing-gowns,' said Run-About. 'There won't be time for you to dress.'

Betty got her tea-set out of the toy cupboard, in its big box. She took the lid off and peeped inside. How tiny the cups were – but soon they would be big enough for her to drink from, because she would be as small as a doll!

Down the stairs – into the garden where the wooden train waited. Once more they became as small as Run-About and climbed into the trucks. Betty still felt as if she were going down in a lift when the Go-Small spell worked!

Off they went at top speed, almost running over a startled hedgehog, and making two little mice squeak in fright. Down the rabbit-hole, hoping not to bump into any running rabbit, and at last out of the other end and into Fairyland itself!

'Oh! Isn't Fairyland beautiful tonight, with the moon shining down brightly?' said Betty. 'And look – that tree is bright with candles! It's like a Christmas tree. Who put the candles on it, Run-About?'

'Nobody. It *grows* candles!' said Run-About. 'If we had time to stop you could pick some. But we really must hurry. Tiptoe's aunt doesn't like to be kept waiting. I only hope she's late!'

They came to Tiptoe's cottage. She had hung it with fairy-lights and it looked very

pretty indeed. Roses and honeysuckle grew all over it, right to the crooked little chimney, and scented the air as soon as they came near.

Tiptoe was waiting at the gate. She ran to meet them, her eyes shining. 'Oh, I'm so glad you've come! And you've brought the tea-set Run-About told me of – oh, isn't it lovely! Just the right size too. We'll soon have the table laid again!'

The seven little sisters twittered round the children like small birds. It was strange to be as small now as they were!

Soon they were laying the table in Tiptoe's cottage, and the two children gazed in astonishment – for there was not a scrap of food there, but only empty dishes. Well, well, well!

'Here's our Aunt High-and-Mighty!' said Tiptoe, suddenly, running into the garden.

Robin and Betty went too. What a strange sight they saw!

A shining golden broomstick was flying high above their heads in the moonlight, and on it rode somebody in a pointed hat and a long and beautiful red cloak that flew out behind in the wind. She pointed the broomstick downwards and swooped towards the garden.

She leapt off the shining broomstick and stood it against the wall. The children stared at her curiously. So this was Tiptoe's aunt, half a witch!

She smiled round and her green eyes twinkled. 'Ha! Quite a party!' she said. 'I hope you've got a meal for me, Tiptoe. I've flown right across Fairyland tonight and I'm hungry.'

'Come in, Aunt,' said Tiptoe. 'This is Run-About the brownie – and this is Robin and Betty, two good friends of ours. Your midnight tea is ready!'

They all went into the cottage. There were not enough chairs to go round the table, so Tiptoe had put two benches at each side, and a chair at each end, one for herself and one for her aunt.

They all sat down. 'Why isn't there anything to eat?' said Robin, puzzled.

Everyone laughed except Betty.

'This is a special meal,' said Tiptoe. 'My aunt once gave me a spell for parties, and I'm using it tonight. We each wish for what we want to eat, and the empty dishes will soon be filled!'

'What a splendid idea!' said Betty, excited. It certainly was fun when they all wished one by one!

'Dewdrop cake!' said Aunt High-and-Mighty. 'Honey buns!' said Run-About. 'Treacle pudding!' said Robin. 'Chocolate ice-cream!' said Betty. 'Mystery sandwiches!' said Tiptoe, and all the seven sisters wished for curious and exciting things too!

A dish was filled by magic each time anyone wished. It really was very peculiar, but the children thought that it was quite the nicest way of getting food for a party. How they enjoyed their midnight meal!

Aunt High-and-Mighty was a most interesting person. Tiptoe said she knew a great deal of magic and had done some extraordinary things. 'Please, Aunt, do tell us a few!' she said.

So the honoured guest told some very strange and mysterious tales, and the children almost stopped eating when they heard them. How they wished that, like Tiptoe, they had an aunt who was half a witch!

Tiptoe's aunt said goodbye at last, and went to get her broomstick. She suddenly turned to the two children. 'I like you,' she said. 'You're nice children with good manners. Would you like me to take you home on my broomstick, just for a treat? Jump on, then – that's right. Hold tight, we're off!'

There they go, up in the air on the shining broomstick – *what* a thing to happen!

Chapter 13

Will Anything Else Happen?

The children sat on the broomstick handle, holding tight with their hands, too excited for words as they flew through the moonlit night. Tiptoe's aunt hummed a little magic song as they went along, and the children suddenly felt sleepy.

'Oh – I'm falling asleep – and I shall fall off the broomstick!' said Betty. 'Please, please stop!'

'I'm falling asleep too,' said Robin, in alarm, and he gave an enormous yawn. 'Please, Tiptoe's aunt, fly down to earth. I know I shall fall off!'

But Tiptoe's aunt took no notice and went on humming more and more loudly. The children's eyes closed. They let go of the

broomstick – they felt themselves falling, falling, falling – then BUMP! They arrived somewhere soft and bounced up and down.

'Goodness!' said Robin, only half awake even now, 'where am I? Oh my bed, I do believe. But – how did it happen!'

Betty had landed on her bed too, but she was too sleepy to think about it. In two seconds both the children were sound asleep, still hearing the humming noise in their dreams.

They were puzzled next day about how they fell into their beds, and even Run-About, who had arrived back in the wooden train, couldn't tell them. 'Tiptoe's aunt knows a lot of very powerful magic,' he said. 'I wouldn't worry about how you got back to your beds, your right size, too, if I were you! You were very lucky to have a broomstick ride, I can tell you! I've never had one in my life!'

'We did enjoy ourselves,' said Betty, remembering the wonderful meal. 'Oh, Run-About – I wish you knew the spell to make food-wishes come true! It would be such fun to have a party like that, and let each of our guests wish for exactly what they liked!'

'I enjoyed those Mystery sandwiches,' said Robin. 'I couldn't guess what was inside any of them, but each one was nicer than the last. I wish I had a few to eat now.'

Run-About grinned, and took them to the doll's house. Inside, on the table, was a little paper bag. He took it and went out to offer it to them. Inside were some of the Mystery sandwiches, left over from the party – but they were very, very small, of course.

'I know enough magic to make them big enough for you to eat, if you like,' he said. 'Tiptoe sent them to you.'

'Oh! How lovely!' said Robin. 'Please do make them big now – as big as you can!'

Soon they were eating the Mystery sandwiches, and puzzling their heads to try and think what was inside them.

'Sardines – egg – tomato – cream – chocolate – pineapple – peppermint – goodness, I can taste all those at once!' said Betty.

'We *have* enjoyed ourselves since you came to live with us, Run-About,' said Robin. 'Life has really been very exciting. I do hope you won't go away yet.'

'I really must go next week,' said Run-About. 'It's been a lovely holiday, I must say – though I've had to do quite a lot of jobs, haven't I – with your help, of course.'

'We've *loved* helping!' said Betty. 'It was lucky we had so many toys that were just what you wanted – the Meccano for the bridge – and the tea-set last night . . .'

'And the kite for rescuing Tiptoe's sisters from the tower,' said Robin. 'And the humming-top came in well for that roundabout.'

'And the aeroplane!' said Run-About.

'And don't forget how useful your doll's house has been to me. I've used it for a proper little holiday house! I shall be sorry to leave it next week.'

'I hope something else happens before you go back to live in Fairyland,' said Betty. 'Things will be *very* dull without you, Run-About!'

'I don't expect anything will,' said Run-About. 'There's nothing much on in Fairyland at present, except the balloon-racing on Friday.'

'Balloon-racing! What's that?' said Robin, surprised.

'Oh, it's rather amusing,' said Run-About. 'You know those lovely balloons that you can blow up? Well, we enter those for the race.'

'But – what happens? Do you just blow about?' asked Betty.

'Well, when they're blown up nice and big, we fix a little basket under each one, and the racers each get into them,' said Run-About. 'Then they all set off at a given moment, and see who can go the furthest before the balloon goes flat, or drifts to earth.'

'It sounds wonderful!' said Robin. 'You do do exciting things, Run-About. Are *you* going in for the balloon-race?'

'Rather!' said Run-About. 'I nearly won it last year. I got a friendly breeze to puff me very hard.'

'Can *we* go and see the race?' said Betty. 'Say yes, Run-About! What time will it be?'

'It's in the afternoon,' said the little brownie.

'We could come!' said Betty. 'Mother's going to see Granny then, and she's not going to take us. We could come!'

'All right. I'll fetch you,' said Run-About. 'But you'll have to look after yourselves, because I shall be up in my balloon. Perhaps you'll bring me luck!'

Chapter 14

Off to the Balloon-Races

Betty and Robin could hardly wait till Friday. They looked out some of the old balloons they had had at their last party and blew them up.

'We'll have a little balloon-race ourselves in the garden!' said Betty. 'You take the two red ones, Robin, I'll have the blue ones. We'll throw them up into the wind and see whose balloons reach the other end of the garden first!'

The wind took the balloons along fast, bouncing and bumping them through the air. Betty's blue one won.

'It won because I had blown it up so big,' she said. 'That's why it won!'

They asked Run-About what colour balloon he was going to race in.

'Yellow,' he said. 'I've got it put away carefully at home. We'll get it on our way to the races.'

When Friday came the children rushed off with Run-About in the little wooden train. They trundled through Fairyland till they came to Run-About's little cottage. There were still no doors to be seen, but Run-About soon altered that!

Just as he had done before, he pencilled a little door in the wall, and hey presto, it was a real door! He knocked and went in.

'Why do you knock?' said Robin.

'Just to see if I'm at home!' said Run-About, and that made the children giggle. He went to a chest and opened the lid. Inside lay a big piece of wrinkled-up yellow rubber – his balloon! He took it out and tucked it under his arm.

'I'm glad I remembered where I put it!' he said. 'Come along – we mustn't be late.'

Out they went, and he slammed the door. It vanished at once. *What* a fine way of making sure that no burglars could get in!

Off they went again in the wooden train

and soon came to the field where the bal-
loon-races were to be held. There were hundreds of little folk there, all very excited.

Run-About went to the starting-point, and
shook out his yellow rubber balloon. 'Are
you going to blow it up?' asked Robin. 'You
will need a lot of breath!'

'Oh – I just pop a Blow-Up spell into the
neck of the balloon,' said Run-About. 'Look!'

He popped a tiny blue pellet into the neck
of the balloon and blew on it. At once there
came a hissing sound and the balloon began
to fill with air!

'I wish I had a spell like that when we give
a party and I have to blow up all the balloons,' said Robin. 'You really do have such
good ideas in Fairyland!'

Run-About turned to watch someone else's
balloon being blown up by a spell. His own
grew bigger and bigger and bigger – simply
enormous! Betty watched it in admiration.
How much bigger would it go? Surely it
would burst if it grew much bigger?

'Run-About – don't you think you ought to
stop your Blow-Up spell now?' she called.
'Run-About swung round to look at his balloon, and he gave a shout.

'My goodness – it'll burst. Stop, Blow-Up spell!'

But he was just too late. The balloon was almost as big as a cottage! It wobbled a little – and then burst with a most tremendous BANG! Everybody fell down flat. The balloon disappeared completely except for a few bits of yellow rubber flying through the air.

Run-About sat up, and tears came into his eyes.

'My beautiful balloon! Why didn't I watch it carefully? Now I can't go in for the race. It was my only balloon.'

'Oh Run-About – I *am* sorry!' said Betty. 'Can't you buy one anywhere?'

Robin suddenly put his hand in his pocket. He had remembered that he had stuffed his and Betty's balloons there, when he had let the air out of them after their little garden race.

'Run-About – have one of mine!' he called, excitedly. 'Look, take this blue one, it blows up nice and big!'

Run-About came over to him in excitement. 'My word – do you mean to say you actually brought your own balloons in your pocket! What a bit of luck. Yes, I'd like that blue one, please – you told me how well it blew away in the wind!'

He pushed a little Blow-Up spell into the balloon's neck, and then blew on it. The children watched it slowly swell up, bigger and bigger and bigger!

'Watch it, watch it!' said Robin. 'Its skin is looking thin now. It may burst!'

But it didn't! Run-About stopped the Blow-Up spell at exactly the right moment.

He ran to get the little baskets that each racing balloonist had to tie underneath with rope. He soon attached his and got into it at the starting-line.

All the racers had to hold tightly to a piece of rope stretched across the field, or their balloons would have gone up into the air at once, the wind was so strong!

'One – two – three – GO!' shouted a voice, and every racer let go the starting-rope.

'Good luck, Run-About, good luck!' shouted the children. 'We do hope you'll fly farther than anyone else. Good luck!'

Run-About's balloon had shot high into the air and the wind took it nicely. Would it win the race? Mind that holly-bush, Run-About! Fly, balloon, fly fast!

Chapter 15

Happy Ending

There came a little rattling noise beside the children, and Robin looked round. It was the wooden engine!

'Oh Betty – the engine wants us to get in so that we can follow the balloons!' said Robin. So in they both got and the little train rattled away over the countryside after the balloons. There were altogether twelve in the race.

Pop! One blew against a pine-tree and the pine needles pricked it! Bang! Another blew against a tall holly-tree and that was the end of that.

A third one began to go down flat, and then two more. 'Only seven left now, and Run-About is second,' said Robin, looking up from the little train.

Bang! Bang! Two more burst. That left five. Then one drifted right down to the ground instead of flying. That left four.

Bang! Oh, dear, was that Run-About's? No, it was another blue balloon that had gone pop. Only three left – and look, one was gradually going down, smaller and smaller. Ah, that was out of the race too.

Now only Run-About's blue balloon was left and a big green one. Run-About was second, but soon a little wind found him and blew him into first place.

The wooden train rattled on, following the two balloons, and behind it came all kinds of coaches and cars carrying little folk who meant to see the finish!

'Oh! Run-About's balloon is beginning to go down – it's getting smaller!' cried Betty, in dismay. She was right – it was already much smaller! Oh, dear!

'The *green* balloon's going down now, too!' shouted someone behind. So it was. What an excitement!

The green balloon kept valiantly up to the blue one, though each was now getting very much smaller, and was drifting down towards the ground. The green one got caught in a bush, and before it could get free Run-About's balloon had gone a good way ahead. But it was going down very fast now, and was a very tiny little thing!

The green balloon sailed on again. The blue one came down to earth, quite flat, and lay there as if it were tired out. Everyone began to shout.

'The green one will win! It's almost up to the blue one. It's winning!'

But no – just a few yards behind Run-About's blue balloon the green one collapsed and dropped down to the grass. It couldn't float even a yard further.

'Run-About's won! The blue balloon has won!' shouted everyone. 'It got further than the green one! Hurrah for Run-About, he's won at last!'

Run-About looked very pleased indeed. He came over to Robin and Betty. 'It was all because of you and your fine balloon!' he said. 'I wouldn't have won in my yellow one, I'm sure. Thank you very much!'

'What's the prize?' asked Robin, as they trundled back to the starting-point in the little wooden train.

'It's a Magic Sweet-Bag,' said Run-About.

'Whatever's that?' asked Betty.

'Just a little paper bag of sweets, which is never empty, however many you eat,' said Run-About.

'What a wonderful prize!' said Robin. 'A sweet-bag that is always full of sweets!'

'Yes – you can wish for any kind you like,' said Run-About. 'Ah – here we are!'

Everyone clapped Run-About as he went to receive the prize. He came straight back

to the children. He held out the sweet-bag, which looked nice and full.

'Here you are!' he said. 'It's for you! You have helped me such a lot while I've stayed in your playroom, and I want you to have this as a little gift from me! You'll love it.'

'Oh, *thank* you, Run-About!' said the children, hardly believing their ears. A magic sweet-bag was never empty – why, there couldn't be a more wonderful present than that!

It certainly was marvellous. The children enjoyed it very much indeed for the next few days. It didn't matter what they wished for – chocolates, toffees, peppermints, fudge – the bag was always full of whatever sweets they wanted!

It was sad to say goodbye to Run-About when his holiday came to an end. He cleaned up the doll's house nicely before he went, and polished the wooden train.

'Please, *please* come and see us whenever you can!' begged Betty. 'We shall miss you dreadfully. When shall we see you again, Run-About?'

'It's my birthday soon, so you must come to my party,' said the little brownie, his green eyes twinkling at them. 'I'll send you an invitation. You'll see me often. If ever I want to borrow any of your toys, I'll come and ask you.'

'Please do!' said Robin. 'And if we want to see you *very* badly, we'll somehow find a way into Fairyland.'

'I'm going now,' said Run-About. 'Goodbye – and thank you for all you've done for me. I've loved it.'

'Take the wooden engine to get back in,' said Robin. Run-About shook his head.

'No. I'll walk down the rabbit-hole, thank you. It's not really very far.'

Off he went, and the two children were sad to see him go. What a wonderful time they had had with him – and what a good thing they had had so many toys they could lend him!

Betty looked as if she was going to cry. But Robin knew how to stop that! He took up the Magic Sweet-Bag and opened it.

'Have a sweet!' he said. 'Cheer up, Betty – we're going to the birthday party – we know the way to Fairyland – and we've got a Magic Sweet-Bag! We're very, very lucky!'

So they are! Don't you think so?